COUNTESS OF INTRIGUE

A NOVEL OF THE TUDOR COURT

ANNE R BAILEY

Inkblot Press

For my love

ALSO BY ANNE R BAILEY

Forgotten Women of History

Joan

Fortuna's Queen

Thyra

Ladies of the Golden Age

Countess of Intrigue

Royal Court Series

The Lady Carey

The Lady's Crown

The Lady's Ambition

The Lady's Gamble

The Lady's Defiance

Bluehaven Series

The Widowed Bride

Choosing Him

Other

The Stars Above

You can also follow the author at: www.inkblotpressco.ca

1

WINTER 1583

"Why do you think Penelope remained faithful to Odysseus all those years?"

It's late. I should be asleep, not trying to strike up a conversation with my old nursemaid. Outside, the storm has abated, leaving the world buried under an ocean white. Perched on my seat by the window, I am entranced by the beauty of it. The garden my mother dearly loves has disappeared. Tomorrow she will complain and I will try to appear sympathetic, but for now I long to press my forehead against the windowpane.

Behind me, Lady Anne Forrester stirs. "What kind of silly question is that? She remained faithful because that is what a good wife ought to do," she says. I don't have to look at her to know she's rolling her eyes.

All in all, she is the most backward woman I know. She may have been the one who taught me how to read and write, but she hates when I try to draw her into debates. She has no interest in plays, poetry, ballads, or even the English Bible. Nor does she discuss philosophers, politics, or the latest fashions. In fact, I suspect she's a secret Catholic. The way she clutches her book of psalms it might as well be a rosary. Maybe she used to be a nun. It's easy to imagine, as she certainly has the stern face for it.

My father would know. He knows everything about everyone. He's made a living out of knowing. We live in a house filled with nothing but secrets. They are the currency we use to keep clothes on our backs and our larders full. Any coin we have disappears into the pockets of hooded men, beautifully clad whores, and lowly page boys. My father runs the largest spy network in all of Europe. He knows everyone's secrets. But it's better to leave some stones unturned.

Lady Anne is warming her hands by the fire. There's a pang in my chest as I regard her. I can't imagine losing her company, Catholic or not.

I feel like a tragic figure out of antiquity, trapped by a cruel fate. I already miss my home and I haven't even lost it. Yet.

Penelope was like this, left to wait year after year for her husband's return. How did she feel when he didn't return to her even after the Trojan War had ended? Did she learn to accept her loneliness? Or maybe she preferred it.

"I imagine she liked being a widow, but when the suitors showed up, she had to play the part of the loyal wife waiting for her husband."

Lady Anne meets my gaze. Her face is taut with

disapproval. "What put such terrible notions inside your head?"

"I'm just saying that it must have been nice to be the sole ruler of Ithaca..."

"She had a son, didn't she? Once he grew up he would inherit his father's kingdom. She was only safe-guarding his inheritance. And you saw what trouble a woman on her own attracts. Penelope was lucky her husband returned."

Lady Anne doesn't use the word *regent* to describe Penelope, as that would give her power. But regardless of how people might try to diminish it, Penelope held power. For a time at least.

Then a thought strikes me and it's hard to keep from smiling. Despite her best efforts, it's clear Lady Anne has been paying attention as I read aloud. "I thought you didn't like the Greeks."

"Heathens," she says. The word comes out as a hiss. "I want nothing to do with them. Look at the ideas they've put in your head."

"Don't blame them. It's my silly mind that is at fault. As you have pointed out, Penelope is the perfect model of a loyal wife, even in this day and age."

"Go say your prayers. You should be in bed. Given my age, I should be in bed." Lady Anne shifts in her seat, but she isn't eager to leave the warmth of the fire.

"In a moment." I turn back to the window before adding, "What do you think it would be like to be out there right now?"

She snorts with derision. "Cold, you foolish girl."

She is right. Only a fool would love this icy barrenness. But I prefer it to all other seasons, especially because of what awaits me in spring: marriage.

To marry for the benefit of her family is the duty of every daughter, but it doesn't stop the feeling of dread from welling up in the pit of my stomach. Knowing your duty and actually doing it are two different things. It's not that I fear the wedding night. That business between a man and his wife does not make my toes curl. Nor does the thought of leaving my family home keep me tossing and turning all night. Not even the uncertainty of childbirth gives me pause.

No, it's him. My intended: Philip Sidney. Even now I can't think of him without my cheeks growing hot from embarrassment.

The last time we spoke my father had just informed me I was to marry him. Sidney was sitting to the left of my father at the dinner table and didn't even bother looking up from his fish.

Then my father had suggested rather calmly that now would be as good a time as any to sign the betrothal contract.

"I agree." Sidney yawned. "Your hospitality has been lavish as usual. Let's conclude this business so I may sleep."

I looked from him to my father, unable to comprehend what I was hearing. "Why on Earth would you wish to marry me?" The question cut through the room, silencing all other conversation. My father fixed me with one of his infamous glares. I never felt so small.

It was Sidney who spoke first. "Lady Frances, I am marrying you so we might form a lasting alliance between our two families." He took his time over each word, leaving no room for any misunderstanding.

Perhaps he thought I was a simpleton. I certainly had not been able to keep my composure and was forced to focus on my hands, squeezed into tight fists in my lap.

Neither my intended nor my father said anything more to me and the pair of them, thick as thieves, left the room.

The memories are still painful to recall. Even my mother's comforting words did little to soothe my injured pride. I had made a fool of myself and I had seen the look of contempt on my future husband's face. If there was ever a good way to start a marriage, this was not it.

All I imagine when I think of Sidney is how he looks past me as if I am not there. When I grow accustomed to this thought my mind comes up with other scenarios, both real and imagined, that torment me. I see him laughing with all his friends at how silly I am, how incompetent. Will he turn away from me in disgust after we say our vows? I cannot imagine this man would ever cherish me.

Why must I marry him?

I pray for guidance as I never have before. He is my father's protégé, the son he never had. Since my father cannot legally make him his heir, he has married him to me, his only surviving daughter. It is a neat solution that benefits everyone but me.

The Sidney family is well regarded and sits high in

the queen's favour. They are famous for being accomplished courtiers and scholars. That is intimidating enough, but they are also wealthy with an impressive family lineage that connects them to the dukes of this realm. Who am I but the daughter of a lowly knight?

Every day I hope that news will arrive from London that Sidney has changed his mind. Then every night as I lay my head down on my pillow I assure myself that tomorrow will be different. Tomorrow I will discover I am no longer betrothed.

It is ridiculous that no one asks me if I agree to the match. The priest might ask on the day of my wedding, but how could I say no and flee back down the aisle? Has anyone ever done such a thing? I recall there were sainted women who fled, but they usually suffered terrible fates and if they did not then they were still not free to do as they pleased.

The bride is an afterthought in this whole marriage business. The glue that seals the deal. And now I can vouch that it isn't a very pleasant experience. Even the promise of a new gown does nothing to cheer me.

"Lady Frances, are you well?"

Blinking, I see Lady Anne is at my side. She places a warm hand on my forehead. "I was just thinking."

"You are so pale and cold. If you catch your death, your father will hang me up by my feet. Come to bed now." Her voice is soothing. Her eyes soften as she regards me. There are many things that we don't discuss out loud. My deep unhappiness is one of them. I must stop this nonsense. How can I be afraid of such a little thing as marriage? Did my father not survive the St. Bartholomew massacres? Am I not his daughter? Giving her hand a gentle squeeze, I obey at last and slide away from the window.

"It wouldn't be by your feet. He would string you up by your wrists. It's just as painful, but you wouldn't die or pass out." In a house like mine, with a father like mine, you learn a thing or two.

She chucks me under my chin as if I was still a child. "Petulant as always."

The next day the sky is clear and the snow already shows signs of melting. The scullery maid has already been in my room, building up a fire against the cold that has seeped in overnight.

There might be time for me to slip down the stairs and out through the courtyard to the stables beyond. The roads might be clear enough for me to manage a ride, even if it's just around the manor grounds.

Just as I finish throwing a cloak over my shoulders there is a tap at my door. Lady Anne is still fast asleep. Sneaking out the back passage is tempting but foolish. There's really only one option.

Carefully, I open the door to reveal Master Sidwell standing there.

He bows his head respectfully to me. "Your father wishes to see you, Lady Frances," he says as he takes in the cloak tied around my neck. He will report to one of my parents what he has seen. There will be questions about what I'm sneaking out to do at this early hour. Or worse, if I'm meeting with someone.

It's almost thrilling to be suspected of something so illicit.

"Very well, where is he?" I ask out of habit. The answer is always in his study.

"I shall escort you, my lady." He bows again.

So he's decided I cannot be trusted. My father has all the people in his employ well trained. He never chooses people who are slow-witted or easily swayed by bribes—though as he reminds me frequently, everyone has a price. He'd rather have a farmer's boy for his secretary than a gentleman's son if he's quick on his feet.

The air is crisp as we walk through the wood-panelled halls of Scadbury Hall. We pass by the portrait gallery occupied by only a handful of paintings. We are not an ancient family established here for generations, nor does my father wish to spend precious gold on something so frivolous.

By all accounts, Scadbury Hall is a welcoming house. We do not turn away travellers and show visitors every hospitality. We feed the poor from our kitchen—proper meals of thick stews and bread, not our table scraps.

My father, who does not believe in waste, will often find employment for these unfortunate souls. He believes, and rightfully so, that it is the duty of a landowner to look after his tenants. A country that cannot look after its poorest inhabitants is not one that can thrive.

He holds the unpopular belief that given the opportunity, anyone has the potential to rise to greatness. We only have to look to our own family history to know this is true. A few generations back we were nothing more than merchants. Even just a few years ago, my father was forced to flee England to escape the Catholic queen and her inquisition. She would have burned all of England down if God didn't intervene and bring Queen Elizabeth to her throne. In a reversal of fortune, my father is now one of her advisors, working every day on making sure the Catholic pope never holds sway in England again.

He loves England and, by extension, the queen so fully there is room for no other in his heart. I am certain she doesn't have a more devoted servant than him. Even so, she often holds him at arm's length and he, desperate for her acknowledgment, continues to do more to prove he is worthy of it.

I suppose that is our family's curse: we are doomed to misplace our affections.

You only have to look at my mother to see this is true. She adores my father to the point of obsession. If he were to die before her, she would journey to the underworld to retrieve him, just like Orpheus did. Except she would not fail. Since they are both still alive and well, she spends her days tending to his every need and hanging on his every word. She waits for him to return her love while paradoxically believing she is unworthy of it. The fact that she has only borne him a daughter, me, torments her. She is never unkind to me, but I catch her frowning at me when she thinks I can't see. I am a constant reminder of her failure to be perfect.

Spiteful as my mind often is, I imagine telling her that even if she gave him ten sons, he wouldn't love her any more.

But that is ungrateful of me. She is hurting as I am hurting.

As I have said, my family is cursed to look for love in the wrong place. That is why I am left pining for their affection. It is an old wound I have learned to live with. After all, I've had a lifetime to grow accustomed to being forgotten by my parents, as if I was a stray afterthought they accidentally wished into being one day.

We arrive at the door that leads to my father's office. Master Sidwell does not bother to knock and instead holds the door open for me.

My eyes need time to adjust to the brightly lit room. We spend a fortune every month on just the candles and lights in this room. My father, economical and calculating, keeps beehives on our property and has our own servants make the candles. He has oil lamps imported from as far as Constantinople.

Many like to imagine he works away like a spider in the dark making its web. Seeing this lavish room would spoil their fun.

"Good day, daughter," he says, getting to his feet.

I bow deeply. "Good morning."

"I am sorry to have interrupted your day. Your mother has spoken to me about ordering you a new gown and making general preparations for the nuptials." He begins what I suspect will be a long speech. As he talks his eyes are trying to pry my mind open for his inspection. I stay very still. "I am afraid I cannot allow it."

He pauses, expecting me to say something. I am uncertain what he wants me to say. But I know as well as him that if there's no money for such finery then there is none. I am as economical as an alehouse wife. Even though I may be young, I'm not the sort to cry over baubles and silks.

"Do you want a drink?" He invites me to sit as if we were equals sitting down to discuss the terms of a contract. My curiosity is piqued, but drawing up the rear is my fear of some recent development.

"No, thank you." Gracefully, I lower myself onto a wooden stool with a worn padded seat.

"Very well. There is no easy way to say this. You are a good daughter to me—you will understand. We cannot make preparations for a wedding or be seen to."

Hope flares and then quickly dies in my throat only to be replaced by a growing anxiety. I feel myself drawn into the spider's nest.

"Oh."

"I hadn't meant to involve you in this."

But he did.

"You will have to marry Sidney in secret. The queen does not approve or would not approve of the union. But we will press on and she will come around. Eventually."

And what if she does not?

The tightness in my chest is growing. My breaths are coming in shallower, and I fear I may faint. To stop myself, I dig my nails into my palms until I fear they have drawn blood.

"You might have to beg for forgiveness from the queen. She will understand. Play the part of the love-struck young woman."

Why would I want to play a part in this charade?

Finally, I cannot continue to sit here as meek as a mouse. "But I do not love him. If the queen would hate this marriage so much, then I do not want to go through with it." I get to my feet, clenched fists at my waist.

He approaches me slowly, his gaze disarming in its sincerity. My father takes my hand in his.

"This is greater than me or you. This is for England's benefit. Bad advisors mislead the queen. I need a strong ally bound to me by more than an oath."

"So you would offer me up to the gods as Agamemnon did his only daughter."

The corners of his eyes crinkle. "I am not asking for your life."

You might as well be. The faintness leaves me and now I am seeing red.

"But you would still see my blood shed."

He does not scold me for such vulgar talk. Gently, he pries my fist open and looks at the wounds inflicted there. He pulls out a handkerchief and bandages my hand. Then he moves on to my other, working with the efficiency and skill of a surgeon. Then, when he is done, he embraces me, enveloping me in the scent of pine, lavender, and horse. The smell of home.

"I know this isn't what you want. But it is your duty

and I will demand you perform it both for me as your father and for your country. Sidney will be a kind husband. I would not give you to a cruel man. You can have all the clothes and jewels you deserve as a new bride after your marriage."

"You know I don't care about such things." I pull away. "Can't I—" But I cannot finish what I have to say. All he is asking is that I play along. A secret marriage would be preferable. I wouldn't have to put up with people fussing over me and teasing me. But maybe there's a chance this whole thing doesn't have to happen.

"If this marriage displeases the queen, she might send you both away from court. Your careers would be over."

He tilts his head, considering me with something akin to admiration. "It's a risk we are prepared to take."

The conversation is over. I don't have the stomach for a fight.

~

The urge to go outside and ride around the countryside has left me. Weary and emotionally drained, I retreat upstairs to my private apartment. As I enter, Lady Anne is busy scolding the maid for making my bed incorrectly. According to her standards the bedcovers are not straight enough.

She stops when she sees me and arches an eyebrow. The poor maid bobs a curtsy, grateful for the interruption.

"Where did you run off to this morning?"

"My lord summoned me." The bile is still in my throat. I cannot bring myself to call him father.

Her gaze travels to my bandaged hands and her brows furrow but doesn't ask. She drops the matter and returns to ordering the poor maid around while I sink into my seat at the window.

We go to the little chapel, hear mass with the entire household, and then return to break our fast in private. Cheese, fresh bread, and mincemeat pies are served to us on platters of silver gilt. My appetite surprises me. When my stomach feels like it might burst, I recline in my seat and sigh, as content as a barn cat.

"Shall we attempt to go for a walk?" Lady Anne suggests, not looking up from her plate.

She's doing me a kindness. I know how much she despises the cold. She is at least ten years older than my mother, who just turned forty, and I know how her joints creak and ache this time of year.

"I shall order the stable master to prepare the sled. We can go for a drive and hide under thick furs and blankets."

She nods.

It's mid-afternoon by the time we are bundled into the sled. The driver clicks his tongue and the horses set off. They are heavy workhorses meant for the plough, but now they are transformed into strong majestic creatures by the matching harnesses decorated with bells. The harnesses were sent from Germany, as was the green blanket hemmed with white fur on my lap. My father's Protestant friends have not forgotten him.

It's a mild winter day, but now that we are moving at such a fast speed the wind whips at my face. The chill is pure bliss.

"What happened to your hands?" Lady Anne asks at last as she takes my hands in hers.

"Some foolishness on my part. Nothing more. I hurt myself by accident. The wedding is to go ahead. That is what he wanted to talk about. Don't worry about me. I am completely resigned to it." Lady Anne doesn't need to know that the queen doesn't approve of this marriage. I'm doing this to protect myself as much as her. If they ever questioned her, she will truly be ignorant. But would it matter? The thought sends a fresh shiver down my spine.

"Are you indeed?"

I can tell from her tone she finds this hard to believe, so I do my best to appear nonchalant.

"He's a good man. I am lucky my father has made me such a good match. With time I'll adjust. I don't have any real objections." I am doing my best to convince us both.

She doesn't comment. After an hour we are forced to return, and I leave Lady Anne to warm herself by the fire.

I shake off my cloak, running a hand over the dark grey wool. My maid waits to pack it away in one of my chests, but I send her for some warm ale instead. The sprigs of dried lavender are displaced as I tuck the cloak away, breathing in deep as the scent wafts up.

We don't have long to dawdle. My mother expects me to join her every day for sewing and reading with her ladies. Today is one of those rare days when we don't have guests and we are left to entertain ourselves. Before

I go to her rooms I remove the bandages from my hands. The half-moon indents have already scabbed over, and with any luck she will not notice them.

Scadbury Hall is not a large sprawling place, so we don't have far to go. The doors of her privy chamber are left open. Her generously sized room has large south-facing windows that provide plenty of light throughout the day. Unfortunately, it also tends to get hot even in the depths of winter. A quick glance tells me my mother is not here. My eyes travel to the closed door at the other end of the room that leads to her private bedchamber and the beautiful closet where she has set up a small prie-dieu.

Taking advantage of the bright light, her ladies sit in a half-circle around one of the large windows as they continue their work embroidering the large tapestry. Each woman has her own little corner that she tends to with needle and thread. It's taken the better part of the year to get this far and there is still so much to go.

Marta, my mother's favourite lady, is the first to spot me and gets up without a word to fetch me a chair. Margery Agote, my mother's impoverished niece, invites me to pick which part I would like to work on. Everyone is watching me, soft smiles on their lips. As tempted as I am to know where my mother is, I hold back the question and sit.

They ask me what I've been doing and comment on my pretty dress. It strikes me how attentive everyone is to me. A conspiracy of kindness. This silent show of support reminds me I'm not alone. My mood lightens considerably. I could laugh at how easy it is to get lost in my thoughts.

I settle on the brilliant blue used for the sky and thread the needle. It's mindless work. A balm that silences any new turbulent thoughts.

In time my mother joins us. There is something about her stiff posture, the redness in her eyes, that catches my attention. She's been crying. I cannot imagine it's over me. But later after we stop our work to eat and drink, she pulls me into her bedroom and closes the door behind her.

"What is it, Mother?" I cannot stand the anxiety of waiting. I was never a patient sort of person and over the last few weeks, any patience I have learned has eroded away.

She sniffs. "I know your father has spoken to you."

"Yes. He has."

"It's not his fault."

"I never said it was."

She paces the length of her room. "He keeps embroiling himself in plots. He needs help. Goodness knows the queen still sits on her throne because of him. The number of assassinations he has saved her from—" She cuts herself off. Even now, just between the two of us, she will not divulge state secrets. "But I thought he wouldn't involve you." She approaches me now. I almost want to take a step back. "You don't deserve to be dragged into this. Especially not to lose your chance for a respectable marriage."

"I thought you said this was a wonderful match for me."

She frowns. Melancholic and worried like this, my mother shows her age and more.

"I didn't think it would be like this for you. So much can go wrong. It would ruin your reputation if..."

"You mean if the queen decides that the marriage never happened? She's done it before, making a whore out of her own cousin, Katherine Grey. So why would she hesitate to have my marriage put aside if she despises it so much?"

My mother's breath hitches. I might have a reputation for being flighty and letting my mind wander, but I am not my father's daughter for nothing. I have inherited that knack for guessing people's thoughts from him.

"Mother, he knows this. Father will have made sure that the marriage will hold. He was the one who dismantled Katherine Grey's marriage, was he not? He will know how to protect me. We must trust him."

My words shock her. Flustered, she twists the belt around her waist in her hands. "I never said I didn't trust him. I worry for him. That is all."

How is it that it falls to me to comfort her? But I do it willingly. I take her hands in mine and squeeze them.

"It will be fine. I don't want a big ceremony, anyway. Nor do I need presents and congratulations. If I can make the two of you proud and be of some use, then I am content."

At last she smiles. "Who gave you such good sense? Still, if this goes wrong for him. Frances, you must do your best for him. Come what may, you must never betray this family. Even if the queen locks you away in the tower."

"I wouldn't," I say, and I mean it. Besides, the queen's best interrogator happens to be my father. Only he could have made Katherine Grey, pregnant with her first child, agree that she was never married and that the man she loved had raped her. He is not only a spymaster but also a conjurer, drawing words and confessions out of people. So I don't fear anyone else. Not even William Cecil, who uses his sweet countenance and condescension to whittle out your private thoughts only to use them against you.

"Your father takes such risks upon his shoulders." My mother shakes her head. "He sacrifices so much."

I cannot help but grit my teeth. Of course her primary concern is him.

Her expression is serious as she studies our entwined hands. "I will make sure this isn't some silly business conducted in the dark."

"But I think that's exactly what Father wants. This marriage is supposed to be a secret."

She pulls her hands out of my grip. "There's a difference between being discreet and being vulgar. I wouldn't want anyone to say you gave yourself to him or eloped." She cups my face and kisses both cheeks.

"Be a good girl," she says, as if I am a child of five.

I nod because I do not trust myself to hold my tongue. I return to my needle and thread and the comfort of knowing that I am not the first woman to marry to please her family.

2

SPRING 1583

Despite my wishes for time to slow down, the season begins to change. The days grow longer. A warm breeze carries in the smell of damp soil and fresh grass. There is a sense of hope and renewal as the trees bud. Animals awaken from their winter slumber and birds fill the air with their incessant song. But for us these are hungry days as our winter stores are depleted. We watch with hungry eyes as our fields are tilled and the seed is sown.

My father is still in London, some fresh new danger to unravel, but he will return before Lent and with him will come my betrothed.

I try not to think of this as I help clear out the weeds and till the soil in the herb garden attached to the house. It may be improper of me to be doing this, but Father approves of such hard labour. He understands that one day we might fall from grace and that it is imperative to learn how to feed ourselves. My father abhors the extravagant lords and ladies of the land who wear their ignorance like a badge of honour. They might always have servants to dress them, clerks to write their letters, but they should know how to do it themselves. In this he is more puritan than Protestant, but I am grateful. Working with my hands often gives me as much pleasure as reading a book.

Lately, it has provided me an interesting respite from a day spent in anxious waiting. I never felt like this before, but after I was told of my impending marriage it feels as though I am waiting for my life to begin. Nothing I do here will matter. Any plan or project I take on will go unfinished. It's sad to think about.

Now that the weather is warmer I take out Jessie, my grey speckled mare, for rides in the nearby woods every morning after prayer. My mother spends her days fretting over the household and preparing for my wedding day. I can see how frustrating it is for her to keep the news a secret.

She goes around the house muttering under her breath and then ordering things to be done with some excuse that my father has requested more nutmeg or an extra helping of sugar and flour.

I must admire how she works, like a mouse squirrelling away food for winter. She collects bits and pieces here and there to complete some mental list she keeps.

Then one day it happens. My father's secretary rides into Kent to tell us that my father is on the way with a few guests.

I try my best not to go pale in front of the household,

although I suspect half of them have guessed already something is happening.

My mother purses her lips and pretends to be irritated. "We shall have to manage. How many rooms will be needed?"

The secretary bows his head and says, "At least six extra. The bishop of Canterbury is among the party of guests."

"What an honour." My mother glances my way for a split second before clearing her throat. "Marta, go speak to the chamberlain and make sure we can accommodate these distinguished men."

Marta leaves the great hall in a huff.

It's a wonderful piece of playacting. As if she hadn't ordered the house cleaned from top to bottom and all the rooms aired out and the linen washed just a week before.

~

Standing beside my mother in a fine russet gown, I feel dwarfed and half hidden by her high starched ruff. So I don't get a good look at my husband-to-be as he rides into the courtyard at my father's side. We all drop into respectful bows as my mother greets her husband.

Grooms appear to take the horses of the gentlemen away before my father turns to me.

He is beaming, but I can see from the dark circles under his eyes he is tired.

"Daughter, are you well?"

"I am, thank you." My eyes are downcast. I prefer

looking at the pebbles on the ground rather than meeting his inquisitive stare.

"My guests and I have had a long journey. We shall adjourn until we can have some supper in the great hall," Sir Francis announces in a surprisingly loud voice for his stature.

I am scrupulous in avoiding looking around at the men who have come with my father. They all seem to know about the impending wedding. Despite my best efforts, it's hard to avoid seeing the sly looks they send my way.

My head held high, I follow in behind my mother like the heiress I am.

At dinner I am loath to discover I am being seated beside Sir Philip Sidney.

He acts like a perfect gentleman and sits by my side, plying me with questions.

I don't know if this irritates me more than if he were to ignore me. It would certainly be less embarrassing.

Musicians have been hired to play tonight, and after the last dish is served servants clear away the tables so there can be dancing. They will expect me to join the fray. My back stiffens at the thought.

Philip Sidney is glancing between me and my father as though wanting to know what he should do.

"May I lead you to the dancefloor?" he whispers to me.

"Not for this dance, my lord. Forgive me, I probably ate too much."

"If you are unwell, you should retire for the evening,"

he says. His tone is kind, consoling. Trying to judge his sincerity, I make eye contact with him for the first time. He has dark, piercing eyes that spark with energy and vivacity. I am intimidated by this handsome man but no longer afraid.

"Thank you, but I don't think I should. It has been a long time since I have had the pleasure of my father's company."

He nods. "It is hard sometimes to always be away from home. But we must go wherever duty takes us."

"You shall spend most of your time in London as well, then?"

He shifts in his seat, setting down the goblet of wine in his hand. "I will be at court for most of the year. Though I suspect the queen has plans to send me abroad."

"Oh." I play with the ruff at the end of my sleeve, tugging the starched material.

He guesses my next question before I have time to say it. "But I would wish for my spouse—if I were to have one—to accompany me. I am not the sort to abandon my family."

"Oh." Again I am caught by his intense gaze. "That is good to know." The words come tumbling forth in a river of unease.

His eyes soften, and his hands move toward my own but dare not touch me before so many witnesses. "You should know when I give my word I do not do so lightly."

This feels like love play, but I cannot bring myself to hope he feels such tenderness toward me. I cannot stand the allusions to our marriage either. Knowing my eager father, it shall take place as soon as possible.

But a secret torturous part of me is pleased Sidney is eager to bring me along on whatever far-flung adventures the queen sends him on. I am even more flattered by the attention he pays me. It is so different from his usual cool behaviour.

When my eyes close that night, it is his eyes I dream of.

~

We have a few days of entertainment in which we go hawking in the morning, play bowls in the afternoon, and fish in the stream in the evening. It is as pleasant as a fairy story. He is nothing like the cruel monster I imagined in my head. I can see why he makes such an outstanding commander. His quiet strength and charm are enough to draw me to him. I find myself eager to trust him. The speed at which my opinion has changed scares me.

On the day of my wedding Lady Anne Forrester helps me dress for what might be the last time. She will stay behind with my mother. This pains me but, she is too old to go gallivanting around England and beyond. Even so, I suspect she is always at the very edge of changing her mind. A familiar face would be welcome, but I don't want to trouble Sidney, seeing as his sister has hired on a household staff for us already.

My mother has given me her court gown. The material is black damask, embroidered with seed pearls. In my hair I will wear a ruby broach my father has brought from London as a wedding present. Behind the ruby setting is a portrait of the queen. I study her obscured features and try to envision the real woman. This is an extravagant gift. I thank him full heartedly.

"It would be the sort of jewel you should wear to court. If you ever found yourself there."

I take the hint and make a mental note not to forget.

My mother enters my room just as the maid and Lady Anne finish arranging my hair into a gold net.

She sighs as she sees me. "You look beautiful, my darling."

I feel my cheeks warm at the compliment. Having lived my whole life in the country and in reclusion studying, I am not used to hearing such flattering remarks. Lady Anne warns me that it is common at court to hear such flowery language and not to let myself fall for tender words.

"Everyone is ready and waiting for you," she says, keeping her tone gentle as she approaches. "You will make your father proud."

"You are too kind," I say in an effort to stop the flood of compliments.

She laughs. "Everyone likes to see a blushing bride." Then pats my cheek. "Don't worry. We arranged everything. The bishop of London himself will be witness to you exchanging vows."

That would intimidate anyone, but it isn't as though I am to be married at Westminster with a large crowd watching me walk down the aisle.

We process from our house to the small chapel built near our house.

Philip Sidney is wearing a handsome suit of yellow silk, with gold buttons and slashed sleeves. Then again, I am quite certain he would look good in anything he wore.

When he spots me he tilts his head in greeting and I return the gesture with a small smile.

Getting married is so simple that I am not even sure it has taken place. We say our vows outside the church doors and then proceed inside for matins. After, we serve wine to the small assembly and then come out to the congratulations of the household. At last we head to the great hall, where a feast is waiting for us. It might not be as grand as my mother would have liked, but there is stuffed peacock and cakes spiced with nutmeg, cinnamon, cloves, and mace. Our guests gobble up the venison pastries and candied fruit served on delicate silver dishes. I study them, watching their seriousness melt away as we continue to ply them with delicacies and alcohol. To the awe of everyone, servants carry in a great marchpane castle. It's set before us on its own table.

Staring at the elaborately carved piece, I know my mother has outdone herself. So much for secrecy. Every merchant will know something was afoot.

"You haven't eaten," Philip Sidney says as he doles out a slice of pie on my plate.

"I have a lot on my mind," I say, too busy trying to catch my father's attention to look his way.

"Don't be worried."

"Of course I am worried." Now I turn to examine

him. There's a flush of colour on his cheeks and I realise how that sounds. "I mean, I am worried the queen will be angry about our marriage. I know she didn't give her permission."

My new husband looks relieved I am not about to run for the first nunnery I can find. Of course, there aren't any nunneries left in England, but that is beside the point. He dabs the corner of his mouth with a kerchief. "She will make a show of being angry, but she will approve of it in the end. It is her way. Besides, our friends have hinted at the possibility of this union to her."

My mouth hangs open. "I thought no one was to know about the wedding."

"It needs to be seen to be secret. That's a very different thing. We are about to do some delicate playacting. Better than anything you've ever seen performed in a theatre. Our marriage will upset the queen, we will beg for her forgiveness, and then she will grant it. It plays out rather smoothly as long as we don't go off script."

"My father said—"

He interrupts me. "I know. We didn't know how she would take it when the contract was first signed. But trust me, you don't have to worry." He gives my hand a gentle squeeze. "Please eat something. I don't want people to think you are unhappy or for you to faint."

"I've never been to the theatre," I inform him before taking a bite of the pie.

He smiles despite the snideness in my tone. "Then I shall have to take you."

This comment, more than anything else, reminds me we are now man and wife. In two days we will leave Scadbury Hall, first for Ludlow Castle to visit his father, and then we will make our way to Penshurst Place, my new home. I will be a great lady with a household larger than my mother's to manage. There is no question of me going to court. Raised in the country as I was, the thought of spending so much time around the queen intimidates me. I will prefer the quiet of the country to the intrigue of court.

Before I know it, I am being led upstairs for the bedding ceremony. It's a subdued affair and I am grateful that no one laughs or cheers. The air in my room is perfumed with scented herbs and the four-poster bed is made up with fresh linen. In only a nightshirt, I get into bed using the heavily embroidered sheets to cover myself. It's far too warm in the room, but it's unclear if it's the heavy covers weighing down on me or just my anxiety. My mother and lady's maids stand in a line to the right of my bed, waiting for the priest to come to bless our marriage bed.

My breath catches in my throat as I hear the distant shouts and hooting of the men approaching. A cavalcade of men burst through the door. My husband gives me an apologetic look. It's hard to tell if his rosy cheeks are from embarrassment or from the wine they pressed us to drink all day.

He stumbles into our bed to a fresh chorus of bawdy jests.

The priest, used to such sights and even worse

language, hushes them with one glare before he says mass and blesses our union.

"Amen," I say and hear it parroted back by Philip at my side.

Everyone is sombre now as they pile out of the room to leave us alone for the very first time.

I had been nervous throughout the day and then anxious as I waited, but now that we are here in this darkened room I feel nothing.

But my mind betrays me and I think of my handsome husband, and imagine his lips on mine. I try to rid myself of improper thoughts.

This is just another thing I have to do and then I can go back to being myself. I think of the books and pamphlets tucked away safely in my trunks. Well-thumbed collections of psalms, translations of Greek philosophers, and poetry.

The weight shifts in the bed as my husband fumbles in the dark.

The wood burning in the grate lets out a round of cracks and pops as the log snaps in half. The scent of pine is heavy in the air, a musky masculine scent.

What does one say on such occasions? What does he expect of me?

Nothing has been helpful, not my beloved books, not my mother, who merely patted my hand and told me that in time I might grow to enjoy these night-time duties.

I blush, remembering that awkward conversation. The last thing I want to imagine is my parents coming together like this.

"Will you miss your home?"

The sound of his voice is dampened by the drawn curtains around the bed, but even so it rings in my ears.

The answer is simple, but I find it hard to speak. Eventually I manage to cough out a "yes."

"Do you need something? I can fetch you some wine or something to eat."

I shake my head. "No, but I am hot. Can we remove some of these covers?"

He laughs. "The furs are a bit much."

"I feel trapped here."

In one swift motion he peels away two layers of covers and I can breathe again.

My eyes have adjusted to the darkness. He is sitting on the bed facing me, looking pensive.

He places two fingers under my chin and lifts my head up so I am face-to-face with him.

"I don't want you to ever feel trapped. Nor do I want an unwilling wife."

His tone is soft and consoling, but it sparks an anger in me. Why did he wait until after we've said our vows to wonder how I felt about this marriage?

He pulls away. He must have seen something of that in my expression.

It's up to me to break the silence. "I don't feel trapped by this marriage. Only by the covers, which you have so kindly rescued me from." Why am I always the one doing the consoling?

My husband is at a loss for what to say. Have I struck him dumb with my brutal honesty? Isn't he supposed to be a famous poet? Maybe his experience lies with willing harlots.

"You are right. That was a foolish thing for me to say. I forget you aren't used to the romantic language of the court. But let's make our own vows now, here under this canopy bed. Tell me without fear of retribution or judgement what you wish from me as your husband and I will tell you what I want."

He lies beside me, his back propped up by the pillows. I cannot bear to look at him as I answer. "I want someone who will provide me with a comfortable home and be gentle with me. Someone who will tell me what is expected of me and not be angered when I cannot guess. I want to be respected as your wife, not by just the servants but by you as well." I blame my honesty on the wine.

He mulls over what I have said. I am lulled to calmness by his steady breathing. "I want a wife who I can trust with my affairs and to manage my household when I am away serving the queen. Someone who will give me heirs, God willing. And be a good mother to them. If my company is distasteful to you, then you don't need to see me often. You shall have your own rooms, and I will only visit your bed on rare occasions."

I swallow down my nervousness at the thought of children. Those are all reasonable expectations, but there's also a methodical coldness to them. Then again, that's not fair considering what I said. In the privacy of my mind I tally up the score. We are at an impasse.

Managing a smile, I nod, meeting his gaze. "Your terms sound reasonable."

He laughs at my seriousness. "I agree with yours as well."

This time when he leans in he places a soft kiss on my lips. A shiver passes over me at the contact. I am enveloped by his scent. Through half-closed lids I see him pull away, smiling as he studies my face. Overwhelmed by my attraction to him, I will him to lean in again. As if sensing my desire, his hand drifts behind my head. His fingers dig into my hair, drawing me closer as his lips press against mine, softly then insistently urging them to open.

It's enough to make me moan. But I don't have time to catch my breath and even less to think about what is happening as his other hand slides down over my thigh.

Instinct drives me to wrap my arms around his neck. He trails kisses down my neckline as his hands stroke my body until I am burning up. I am as taut as my lute strings and he uses those expert hands to draw out music from my lips. I don't want this feeling to end. He continues tormenting me. From deep within me, a yearning cry for more goes out. Being pressed down on the sheets beneath his strong body of corded muscle as his hands caress me is pure bliss. I am adrift in a sea of desire.

When he takes me for the first time, I am utterly lost to the sensation. The pain dissipates and I feel a delicious heat pooling beneath my thighs. I am the first to shift beneath him, desperate for something I cannot voice. He moves against me, setting a slow steady pace that both excites and frustrates me.

At last I cry out against him as a wave of pleasure hits me and he buries his face in the nape of my neck.

We are quiet as we sit there wrapped in each other. I am too dazed and embarrassed by what has happened between us to speak.

As he sighs against my neck, the feel of his breath on my sensitive skin sends a fresh wave of goose bumps over my skin. I come crashing back to earth and can't even begin to process what just happened. Now that we have stopped I feel the growing dull pain between my legs.

He pulls his weight off me.

"Did I hurt you?"

I can't answer him. I'm too busy blushing from head to toe.

"I promise I won't come to your bed often..."

He cannot see me, but my mouth is open forming an "O." I am a mess of emotion as I watch him pull back the curtains and walk around the room. He hasn't looked at me. I am just as desperate for him to return as I am terrified.

The fact that he thought this sort of attention would trouble me is just another confusing thought I will need to sift through. Can I admit to him I enjoyed this encounter? If I were a brazen woman, I would call out to him and put matters straight. As it stands, I retreat within myself, shy and skittish as a doe. My old fear that I have done something wrong returns and my hands wring the thin sheet covering my nakedness.

The sounds of him washing fill the room, followed by the rustle of fabric as he dresses himself. Then he pulls back the curtain again, handing me a cup of strong ale. In one great sweep he takes in my wide-eyed expression.

"I have frightened you."

"No." I wish to be open with him. "I—I am confused. I didn't think it would be like this. It felt...pleasant." His eyes are studying me so intently I don't know how I will bear it. My hands clench into tight fists on my lap as I find the gall to say, "Please don't leave."

Silence.

Curiosity gets the better of me. Through my lashes I can see his face is a blank, unreadable slate as he nods. "I won't go anywhere. Besides, it's expected we will spend the entire night together. I am glad you are well. You might wish to clean yourself."

I get up and see the sheet beneath me is stained. Fresh embarrassment wells up inside of me, but without a word he pulls off the cover to reveal a clean one underneath. The soiled sheet is bundled and thrown somewhere near the foot of the bed, out of sight.

I slip my discarded linen shift over my head, wondering when it had been taken off. What happened between us feels like a lifetime ago. I scrub myself at the water basin and drink the ale before returning to the bedside.

There's something cold in his demeanour as I slide back between the sheets. I hesitate a moment until his eyes meet my own. They soften as he shifts to make more room for me.

"Come. I won't bite."

Memories of his teeth on my skin remind me this isn't quite true, but I comply.

He is trying very hard to school his features. What is going through his head? Anxiety rears its hideous head, coiling around my throat.

"We should sleep. Tomorrow will be another long day, and then we will have to travel."

He turns away, rolling on his side, his back to me. There's a pang in my chest. I feel so alone.

"Have I—" I blink away the thought. I am not about to be a whimpering, besotted woman. "Is something wrong, husband?" The question rolls off my tongue with confidence.

"No. I am tired."

Though that is believable, something still doesn't sit well with me. I know he is holding back something.

I think back to what he said before he began trailing kisses down my neck. He didn't speak of love; I didn't expect him to. This play between the sheets was nothing more than a means to an end. I am grateful he wasn't methodical about achieving his ends. There are plenty of stories involving unbearable pain and screaming on the wedding night. By comparison, mine was heavenly, so why am I uneasy?

It must be his sudden strange behaviour that puts me on edge.

I settle myself on my pillow and force myself to close my eyes. "Good night, husband."

"Good night, wife" comes the reply. He chokes on the

word *wife* and I wince, remembering the rumours he had once loved another. Could it be possible he still loves this woman? And if he did, why did he not marry her?

There's so much to ask, but I will have a lifetime with him to unravel these little mysteries. I remind myself once more that I had no expectations when I said my vows.

~

The next day they subject us to rounds of awkward teasing and allusions to the wedding night. The dirty sheets have been cleared away. I am bathed in jugs of hot water, and scented oils rubbed into my hair and skin wipe away all traces of him.

He goes hunting with my father while I return to my mother's rooms. They all watch me with curiosity clear on their faces. By now they must all know that I have done the deed. The thought that they might wish to hear the details fills me with a deep embarrassment.

I offer to read from my mother's favourite book of psalms and thus I am saved from whispered inquiries and chatter.

At mealtimes we are seated together side by side. More toasts are made to our good health and happiness. He smiles as he takes his seat and is courteous to me. I cannot help but wonder if I am imagining the tension between us.

"How was your day?"

His shoulders stiffen and I know I am not imagining

things. He is forcing himself to smile as he replies. "It was lovely. The deer park is well stocked."

Again I am tempted to ask what is wrong, but now is not the time. So, like a dutiful wife, I smile in reply and offer him some bread.

That night he doesn't come to my bed.

At the very least I know our marriage will not be dull if he keeps me guessing like this. I pull the covers up to my chin. An image of my mother clinging to my father springs to my mind. I cannot become like her. I must protect myself even as my treacherous mind reminds me of the pleasure he introduced me to.

He wants heirs, that is all.

We entered this marriage as part of a business arrangement. It would be disingenuous to think that affection after one night would spring between us. He has had countless lovers, even previous engagements if rumours are to be believed. I breathe in deep. I shall learn to be like Penelope, content with ruling my little kingdom. The muscles in my body become loose. There is something satisfying about imagining myself as a shepherdess tending to her flock. I imagine chasing sheep around the hills of Penshurst Place. I close my eyes and think of pastoral bliss. But it is the unbidden thought that love might one day grow between us that finally lulls me to sleep.

3

SPRING 1583

We are leaving Ludlow behind. The towering castle was as imposing as it was freezing. Instead of riding at my husband's side I am resting in a litter like an invalid, my nose running and my head throbbing.

Philip offered to delay our departure, but I was sure another night spent in that cold castle might kill me. Besides, after what feels like weeks adrift on the road I am excited to see my future home at last.

Philip has proven to be a man of his word. He has been nothing but kind to me. Yet he remains distant and keeps our relationship confined to benign pleasantries and the occasional night-time romp beneath the sheets. He never fails to leave me breathless. Despite my best efforts, it is hard to maintain an air of detachment around him. While I accept there might never be love between us, I wish we will become friends. I imagine a day when he will trust me enough to confide in me.

During my illness I received his full attention and kindness, but he doesn't appreciate shows of affection in public or private. He wants to keep our relationship how it is now.

Once, in the throes of passion, I screamed out his name. He silenced me with a hard kiss lest the servants come running and then pulled away. I apologised, though I am not sure why. He patted my bare shoulders. Then, kissing my forehead, he told me he was tired and would go to sleep. I was still half dazed with desire as he left. Anger pulled me out of that fog as I tried to swallow down my disappointment. My pride was hurt and I swore I would speak to him about it. By morning I was a coward again.

The next time he came to my bed I didn't call out. I didn't even call him "husband" when I bid him good night. I hated myself for that.

A sneeze rattles me and brings tears to my eyes. I cannot wait for this cold to pass me by. We are passing through pastures. The blades of grass have been left to grow tall, and wildflowers have sprung up all over the field. It's beautiful here, but we do not stop for a picnic despite my dearest wish. We have a long way to go before our first stop.

"I promise you can have as many picnics as you desire at Penshurst Place," Philip says to reassure me.

I shrug as if it means nothing. I don't say that my father would never let a chance pass him by. Seize the moment, he would say. Nor do I point out that at Penshurst I won't be able to have a picnic with him.

We have settled for the night at a roadside inn. Alone in a dark room I dream I am in a wheat field beneath a clear blue sky and he materialises behind me, pulling me closer into his embrace.

I wake with the taste of bile in my throat and spend the morning mass chastising myself for being so silly. I peek at him at my side. His head is bowed in prayer. Even after days on the road he is handsome. I can forgive myself for my weakness. What woman would not be attracted and half in love with a ruggedly good-looking husband like him at her side? I worry I will break my heart over him, and there are more practical things for me to worry about.

By the time we arrive at Penshurst Place I have wrestled and defeated both my emotions and my cold. Relieved that I am well enough to ride at my husband's side, I try my best to appear composed and dignified. It's hard to keep from craning my neck to get a better view of the house.

"You will have plenty of time to explore," Philip says.

I've been caught, but I toss my head back, determined not to be embarrassed. "It's natural I should be curious to see it."

"And what is your critical opinion? Do you prefer Scadbury Hall?"

It's a gorgeous building. Far grander than the home I have left behind. I can see why the queen would condescend to visit this place.

"I will always prefer the place I've called home all my

life. However, I can tell just from the exterior that this might take second place."

The corners of his mouth twitch in amusement.

The horses' hooves clipping and clopping echo around the courtyard as we come riding in at a leisurely pace.

A grand lady waits to greet us. I know this must be his sister, the famous poetess and patroness of the arts. She is impeccably dressed in a gown of shimmering brocade. The hem of her neckline is studded with diamonds and her wired ruff is magnificent. She wears this outfit with nonchalance at its extravagance. I cannot look away from her as she approaches, floating weightlessly towards us as we hop down from our saddles.

At that moment, musicians spring up and delight us with beautiful song.

Philip is grinning at the surprise and pulls me along to introduce me.

"Countess of Pembroke, allow me to introduce you to my new wife, Lady Frances."

She bows the smallest of curtsies to the both of us and we return the courtesy. Then she sweeps me into her arms and kisses both my cheeks before doing the same to her brother. I smell her sweet perfume and find I am completely entranced by this elegant woman.

"I hope the weather held. It's been raining here constantly," she sighs. "I was afraid I wouldn't be able to greet you properly, but my prayers were answered."

Philip chuckles, shaking his head. "You should pray

for good weather on behalf of our poor crops, not for your musical entertainments."

Unabashedly, she invites us inside as if it is her home and not ours. She does this with such politeness and ease that I cannot fault her. Compared to her I am a stranger here.

As expected, the building is grand and tastefully decorated. The large windows allow for ample sunlight to light the corridors and halls. Scadbury Hall feels like a sad little farmhouse by comparison.

His sister, Mary, sends Philip off to get washed and change into fresh clothes.

He hesitates, looking at me.

"I'll look after her," she assures him, taking my hand in hers.

We are left alone in the great hall. She turns her gaze to me. Her eyes are kind as they sweep over me. I am reminded of my father in how she studies me.

"Don't worry, I will get out of your hair soon. I am just staying for a few days. Philip asked me to ensure you would arrive at a household in good working order." She says this with a wave of her hand. "So I hope to see you settled into your new home by the time I leave. Let me show you to your apartments. I hope you like how I've decorated them."

"I'm sure I will." This isn't a lie. Judging from her sense of fashion, I would say I'm in expert hands.

She takes me to the west wing of the house, pushing open the double doors to my presence chamber. I have a set of four rooms for my use. It feels excessive to know that they are large enough that I would be perfectly content if I was never allowed to leave them.

Beyond the presence chamber, there is a smaller, more intimate chamber. A large walnut table surrounded by chairs dominates the room.

"My mother used to enjoy us having private family meals here. It was rare we were ever together and she wanted us to enjoy every moment we could."

"I can tell you are a very close family," I say. "Philip speaks fondly of you."

"Strange, isn't it, that we all seem to get along." She chuckles. "I know plenty of people who aren't half as lucky. But if you can't trust family, who can you trust?" She gives me a sidelong glance as if she wants to ask me something, but she holds her tongue.

"You can remove the table if you wish. Maybe you have other ideas for the room," she says as she leads me at last to my bedchamber.

A large canopied bed is waiting for me. I smell the scent of fresh dried herbs and air, a tell-tale sign the room has recently been cleaned. Everything from the curtains to the tapestries hanging on the wall is spotless. I don't have to touch the fabric to know everything is of the highest quality. I should expect nothing less, but I am still surprised by the lavishness of it all.

"There's a door behind that tapestry over there." I look in the direction she's pointing to the delicately worked unicorn. "The servants sometimes use it, but mostly my parents used it."

She can see the question in my eyes and explains. "It

connects this room to my father's old ones. They could move between their apartments with no one knowing. When Queen Mary I was on the throne, I'm pretty sure they used it to hide their Protestant priest from the inquisition."

My mouth is dry. "Ah."

She tilts her head to the side, a coy smile on her lips. "Or, if you prefer, you can always keep the door locked. Then you wouldn't be bothered by any night time visitors."

I must be beet red. My skin certainly feels like I'm burning up.

Her face falls. "I'm sorry. I didn't mean to tease you. My tongue always gets me into trouble."

"There's no need to apologise," I say, trying to get a hold of myself.

Lady Mary clears her throat and moves around the room pointing out certain items and their history. These are not just decorative pieces of furniture or items to be replaced but important family heirlooms to be treasured. For instance, there is the screen painted by her grandmother and a great gold clock that came as part of her mother's dowry.

I appreciate how she takes the time to tell me this without being condescending. My heart warms to her and I imagine we could be friends.

"Would you like time to rest, or should I introduce you to your household?"

I hesitate. On one hand, it would be the first step to feeling like less of an outsider, but on the other I don't feel like myself. "Could I have a change of clothes and a quick wash?"

Her eyes are alight as she remembers something. "I think you will enjoy this," she says, eyes full of mischief as she leads me through a third door and out into a short gallery that leads to another room.

We step through, our shoes clicking on the tiled floor. The floor is covered in mosaic tile, but what dominates the room is a large wooden tub with fresh linen.

"I could have them draw you up a proper bath," Lady Mary says. There is a cabinet near the window, and she unlocks the door with one of the many tiny keys she has attached to her belt. She steps aside to reveal jar after jar of perfumes and oils. "I arranged a small wedding present for you."

It's really too much. I open and close my mouth, searching for the right words. She laughs at my incredulity.

"You deserve to be pampered. I know what it is like to be a new bride, torn away from home. Some comforts might ease the transition."

"I will wash, but a bath would be too much."

Lady Mary looks disappointed, but she shrugs. "If that is what you wish."

I rush to add, "And thank you. This is all amazing. You are very generous."

A smile spreads across her face. "I am trying to make you feel welcome. It wasn't too long ago that I was in your shoes, and my experience was less than..." She snaps her fingers as she tries to pick the perfect word. "Satisfactory."

The urge to ask her what she went through bubbles up in my chest, but I don't know her. It would be presumptuous. Lady Mary is kind, but everything about her also makes me feel deficient. I am not as graceful, not as well dressed or well spoken. I have never felt like more of an inexperienced country girl than now. Exhaustion is creeping into my bones as the adrenaline of seeing Penshurst Place is dying down.

"I will summon a maid to help you," she says, her eyes scanning my face before she leaves. I am alone in the tiled room that now feels so cold.

A moment later a young woman appears carrying in a large jug of hot water. She bobs a curtsy, not spilling a single drop, and introduces herself as Matilde.

Two more follow in behind her, one carrying towels and the other fresh clothes.

They peel away layer after layer of clothing. At least my riding gown is uncomplicated and I am free of it in moments. Only the bodice of the gown is decorated with gold braid. The high neck is etched with white lace that is removable to make it easier to wash.

I take my time deliberating which scent I should wear and settle on mint and thyme, which is added to the water before I sponge away the dirt and grime of weeks of travel and sickness. I rub the skin on my face raw before letting Matilde comb the tangles from my hair. She is methodical but gentle, and when she is done my dark hair is glossy and falls down my back in gentle waves.

The gown they have laid out for me is tan in colour with a black bodice and hemline. It's beautiful, and decidedly not one of mine. Next time I see Lady Mary I will ask where these gowns come from.

My hair is pulled up into a net and kept in place with silver pins. When I am older perhaps I will opt to wear the caps I have seen my mother wear, but I cannot bring myself to do so. In this magnificent house I would rather not appear to be the scullery maid.

I am investigating my presence chamber when Lady Mary returns.

"You are transformed," she declares with a flourish of her hand. "I almost didn't recognise you. Let me take you for a proper tour now."

Following behind her is a tall dignified man.

"This is Mister Jonathan Smith, the steward who's been managing Penshurst Place for my brother. He's been a most loyal servant. You can trust him with anything."

As he bows I can see the slight reddening of his cheeks and his mouth pursing in embarrassment. Lady Mary's forward way of speaking seems to have that effect on many people.

"At your service, my lady."

My response is a simple nod, mainly because I am stunned into silence and still new at being in command of my own household. It should've been easier for me, given my upbringing, but comparing myself to Lady Mary with her assured confidence has made me lose any that I had tucked away.

We roam Penshurst Place, Lady Mary handing over the ring of keys she possesses to locked cabinets and desks where precious possessions are kept as we do so. The keys are heavy on my belt and I know it shall take me a long time to remember what each is for.

Finally, we meet the ladies who are to make up the bulk of my household. They had been instructed to keep out of my way until they were summoned.

Lady Askew is the third daughter of a local knight. Her mother was a distant relation of the Dudley's and is highly born enough to be my companion. Among the other three ladies, only Marianne looks to be about my age, but they are all genial and pleased to be introduced to me.

Beyond these ladies who will be my companions and help me dress and take care of household tasks, I have two maids who will help keep my rooms tidy and a scullery maid to remove the chamber pots and ensure the fireplace is kept clean and lit.

My new life as a country wife will be busy organising the household accounts, managing our food supplies, and entertaining my husband and his friends if they were to visit. This might even include the queen. A thought that fills me with terror and excitement at the prospect of such a challenge.

Finally, Lady Mary drags me out to one of the many gardens, where she has ordered a great meal to be laid out for us among the newly budding roses and posies.

My husband joins us, looking refreshed. A thrill of pleasure passes over me as he does a double take when he sees me. Lady Mary catches it and gives him a wide teasing smile.

"As you can see, I have taken good care of your wife," she says. "Maybe next time you won't be so eager to part from her company."

Philip clears his throat and fixes her with a look that silences her. "It is the nature of our lives that keeps us separated." He turns to me, his dark eyes searching mine. "I will be leaving for London soon."

He doesn't offer any apology.

"Of course. If there's anything you need me to do, let me know." My voice is a whisper as I try to hide the inkling of disappointment. I really shouldn't feel anything but relief that I will be left to my own devices but, alas, here I am.

He sits at the table, examining the plate and cutlery with a critical eye. "This would be good enough for the queen," he says, a raised eyebrow at his sister.

She shrugs innocently. "A celebration of my own since I couldn't be at your wedding."

Indeed, we eat as well as if it was a fine feast, even though this is an intimate meal for the three of us. There is roasted venison, stuffed chicken, drowned in a sauce of currants and wine, and far more cakes and puddings. I pick at my food, my stomach unsettled by the richness of it all.

Even as Lady Mary presses me to eat more, I cannot bring myself to.

"She eats lightly." My husband comes to my rescue.

"Or is it your company that makes her shy?"

I balk at her biting remark. Now I wish to disappear.

Philip doesn't even glance my way as he says, "Then she shall eat better once I am gone."

"What a poet you are," Lady Mary says with all the sarcasm she can manage. Then she looks at me with a kind smile. "I am sure you shall whip him into shape sooner or later. You must forgive him for being so cold-hearted."

I look between the two of them, trying to make sense of their relationship, which on one hand is close but on the other is confrontational. There are too many secrets even for me, the daughter of the queen's spymaster, to unravel.

"He's been nothing but kind." Philip still doesn't look my way and I return to picking at the food on my plate. Of all the things I do have an appetite for it is the custard topped with preserved apples.

The siblings move on to talk of other things. I listen, enthralled by the news that Mary, Queen of Scots, is plotting some fresh trouble. She is a great enemy of my father, even though I doubt the two have ever spoken, but he hates her above all other Catholics. She represents a great threat to England as a Protestant nation. If she were to inherit the English throne, as it seems likely our Queen Elizabeth will never produce an heir of her body, then she might seek to bring us back to the Catholic fold. Just a few years ago another Queen Mary tried to do just that, and it ended in bloodshed and innocents perishing in terrible ways.

My father, who, alongside my husband, witnessed

the St. Bartholomew massacre of Protestants in France, will do anything to make sure she never sits on the English throne. Her presence in England has already brought our nation nothing but grief. But now that she is here we cannot risk releasing her, nor can we risk killing her without bringing down the anger of France and Spain upon us.

It is my father's job to help navigate these treacherous waters and advise the queen on what she should do.

I am sure he would prefer to see her dead, but he would also not wish to risk drawing England into a war we cannot win. Not to mention that the nation is always on the verge of bankruptcy, despite the queen's careful budgeting.

An alliance would surely solve our problems. But the queen will not be forced. She values herself too highly to tether herself to a man. I both admire her for this and hate her for it. It's confusing and uncharitable of me.

That night, as I send off my ladies to sleep in their own adjoining bedrooms, I hear a tap at my bedroom door. In steps my husband a moment later, papers in hands and an exhausted look on his face. Gone is the pale grey suit he wore earlier today. Instead, he is dressed in a thick robe and likely a night shift underneath that.

He places a kiss on my forehead before sitting down before the fire and I watch him feeding the papers in his hand one by one to the flames.

Why?

"Please forgive my sister," he says with his back still turned to me. "You will get used to her eccentricities soon enough. Tomorrow I am leaving as early as possible, and she shall leave the day after. You won't be alone. There will be plenty of help if you have any questions, and you need not do anything except wait for my summons."

"That sounds rather dull," I say. My tone is light, as though I'm making a joke rather than scolding him internally for assuming I'd be happy to sit around doing nothing.

Silence.

"What were those?" I ask, though I'm really wondering why he came to my room solely to burn them. Perhaps my fire is the best there is in all of Penshurst Place. That brings a smile to my lips and I have to hold back a laugh.

He's turned to look at me and it's too late to hide the smile. His eyebrows shoot up.

"Correspondence I want to make sure no one else can read. I was going through them but then found myself at your doorstep. I am sorry for being so distracted. My mind is in a million places..."

His brows crease and I realise how tired he looks. I approach my husband with small tentative steps but then bravely wrap my arms around him.

He stiffens at first but then releases a breath and leans against me, his head pressed into my stomacher.

"You are tired." I am stroking his hair, thinking it's unfair that any man should have such thick silky locks.

"Don't worry about me. I'll be fine. I can also help you if you wish."

"I know I am neglectful." His words are muffled by the fabric of my dress. "I nearly left without speaking to you."

I am surprised by the tightness in my chest and nearly stop the gentle strokes, but I don't want him to know the words hurt me.

"Do you want to go to bed?" I try my best not to make it sound like a proposition. I can feel how tired he is. We have both been away from home for far too long.

He nods against me.

His robe is off and I join him after dismissing the maid.

We do nothing but sleep until the first signs of dawn stir him. He places a kiss at the nape of my neck and my eyes flutter open.

"I know it's early, but I thought—once more before I left. If you were carrying a child, then..."

"You'd be happy," I finish for him.

He nods and I turn toward him, pulling him close. In that moment I try to ignore the fresh questions blossoming in my chest. Does he come to my bed for duty alone? Is our coupling such a chore for him? Regardless, I do my duty. I remind myself that he is a good husband to me. He is considerate. I should be grateful he's not a fumbling buffoon pawing at me in the dark. But I hate to be reminded by these little comments that we are nothing but strangers.

When he is done he slips on his robe and regards me sitting up against the headboard.

"Take care. Write to me if you need anything," he says, coming forward to kiss me.

In exchange, I give him my wifely blessing. I should be in the courtyard watching until he disappears over the horizon with his retinue. But I can see he doesn't want to make a fuss. He will slip out of our home now that he has done his duty in depositing me here.

Once he is gone, I let my head sink back into the down-filled pillows and sleep.

The sun is bright overhead by the time I wake. No one woke me, but I don't mind. I shall go pray in the chapel on my behalf.

Lady Mary is wandering around outside, losing herself in the hedgerows, paper in hand.

I am sorry to interrupt her, but when she sees me she smiles and calls out.

"I was wondering what was keeping you this morning. My brother has left us." She gives me a sidelong glance, as though she isn't sure how I will react.

"I know," I reassure her.

"Oh." She is genuinely pleased to learn that. "I was afraid he might have snuck off without a word to you." She reaches for my hand, patting it as if I need sympathy.

My suspicions are alerted, but I try to push my worries aside. I don't care. I can't. It isn't fair to either of us.

"You have a harsh opinion of your brother," I say,

letting her pull me along on the garden path. New life is springing up everywhere.

"He's a poet," she says, as if that were to explain everything.

"As are you," I point out with a smile.

"Ha. True. But I do fear he is far more emotional than me. Don't repeat that to anyone else," she says, and I promise her I won't.

"He didn't wish to marry me?" I guess.

She shakes her head but now looks eager to change the topic. I don't want to drop the topic.

"I wouldn't like to be the last to know. If there is anything to know." I am as vague as possible, for I cannot voice my worries that my husband has made other secret marriages or has fathered children with other women. While I might feel hurt, the thought of such messiness worries me more. I don't want my children's inheritance to be divided up among his bastards.

"There is nothing you need to concern yourself over. He married you."

Meaning there were other offers on the table. Maybe ones that appealed to him more, but then he must have settled on the advantageous marriage to me. I say nothing of this to her, but I understand enough. She's right. I don't want to know more. There's no need for me to know more. I am his lawful wife unless the queen finds a way to separate us.

"He told me you were departing tomorrow as well." I change the topic smoothly.

"Yes, I am afraid business cannot wait." She winks

and hands me the paper she was holding. "I've been working on a play. But as you can see I am stuck."

The parchment is splotched with ink, and scratched-out words make it hard to read. I give it back to her when she sees my pained expression.

"It's a disaster." She nods.

"I wouldn't say that. Just hard to read."

"You should've seen my first draft."

We both laugh. The weather proves to be a perfect day and she takes me riding around the Penshurst park. There will be a lot for me to explore once she is gone. My husband keeps a well-stocked stable and there are horses for all my ladies. I prefer hawking to hunting, and she takes me to the mews where a handful of birds are being taken care of by a hawker.

"This is Morgana." Lady Mary points to a hawk with feathers strangely speckled. "A beautiful if particular creature. She belongs to my brother. I am sure he will not mind you taking her out."

I stroke her pale belly. The feathers are like silk. I glance down at her talons and see they are long and sharp. She would be a force to be reckoned with out on the field.

"Philip hand-raised her. They were going to kill her because of her strange colouring, but he saved her from such a tragic fate. She's proven to have been worth the effort. One of the deadliest and fastest birds I've ever seen. Philip was thinking of gifting her to the queen, but he cannot part with her."

"I can see why." Despite the uneven markings, she is

stunning. "I shall make sure she doesn't get bored while he is gone. Frankly, I am surprised he doesn't take her to court with him."

"He likes to travel light," Lady Mary says.

Humming, I take a step away from her and watch as she preens her feathers. We are both alike, two women tucked away for safekeeping. I think of Circe, trapped on an island yet becoming a powerful sorceress despite the other unsavoury side to her. Or Helen of Troy, who escaped her loveless marriage to find love in the arms of a Trojan prince. Maybe it was selfish of her to not care that she caused such a tragic war, but I admire she put her desires first.

It's with a heavy heart that I bid Lady Mary farewell. She is an intimidating presence, but she is kind and someone I could lean on.

Now that I'm the lady of the house I have free rein to do as I please. Time to roll up my sleeves and get to work.

4

SUMMER 1583

For all of the season of Lent I am left to my own devices. I take it as a compliment that I am trusted to manage a household of my own. Of course, my husband has left me in the capable hands of his servants and advisors. I am sure they report everything that happens to him.

Lady Mary chose well for me. My ladies are all women who I could be friends with, but I have grown the most attached to the youngest of my ladies. She is abrasive and speaks her mind. I should scold her and set a better example for her, but I laugh instead.

We ride around Penshurst Place to oversee the fields as the crops grow. A dusting of green replaces the barren earth. This spring, the weather has been perfect. I lead the house in a mass of thanksgiving that so far the signs are good for a healthy harvest. We will not go hungry this winter.

I am sad to learn there are no sheep being raised at

Penshurst, and when I make the suggestion that perhaps some can be bought the steward smiles and assures me he will look into it.

"Just know that wheat has always been our most profitable crop," he says. "There's the fruit orchards as well. You wouldn't want to rip those out to make room for some sheep, would you?"

I cannot argue with him, at least not yet. A while later I remember with some indignation that I am the lady of this manor. My command supersedes that of the steward. However, I cannot just exert my will without burning bridges. I should foster loyalty, not antagonising would-be allies. Like my father before me, I know I must tread the path of diplomacy.

I take up pen and paper and do some calculations. My foolish dream of chasing sheep in the meadow has evolved into a chance to prove myself and exercise some power. I should be content to sit in my room and enjoy the simple pleasures life has to offer, but I have inherited my father's ambition. But I'm capable of more. I survey my husband's lands and remind myself they are now mine as well. A few good acres around Penshurst make up my dower.

The area has a few cottages rented out to tenants. But there is plenty of common land. I bite my thumb as I consider the cost of building barns and acquiring sheep. I consult with builders and speak with the tenants.

In the end, I have what I need. This time when I approach the steward I have my figures ready. I don't ask but rather tell him of my plans. At the very end, I wait to see what he will say. I have not commanded him to do anything.

To his credit, he doesn't criticise me, nor is he put out by the fact that I ignored his hint that this isn't a good idea. He raises his eyebrows as he looks over the papers I hand over to him explaining that most of the tenants have agreed to take on the responsibility of caring for the sheep. In exchange, they will keep a percentage of the wool and one lamb in every five.

"They would not deny the lady of the house," he points out.

"True, but I gave them options. I said I had been thinking of chickens as well."

He adjusts his cap and grins. "Then everything is settled. Give me your orders and it shall be done."

Without any hesitation I pull out another folded piece of paper. He breaks the seal, and his eyes fill with mirth as he finishes reading and looks back to me. "You've put a lot of thought into this, my lady."

"I have."

"I apologise for how that sounds. I shouldn't have expected anything less from a noble lady."

He is flattering me, but I feel my face flush nonetheless. "You weren't wrong. When I first spoke with you it was a foolish whim, but after I investigated the matter it is clear that we could raise sheep on our land. Any surplus wool could be sold for a tidy profit while the rest would provide us with plenty for our daily needs."

He bows at the waist. "Consider it taken care of, my lady."

After he leaves I take a deep breath in. For the first time in a long time I feel confident. It's not hard to imagine carving out a future here.

The summons to come to court arrives at the beginning of May. I am urged to hurry, as the queen will be departing for one of her famous summer progresses soon.

Old anxieties tighten around my throat until I find it difficult to speak. In the mornings, I am ill, and throughout the day I am sluggish.

Then, a day before leaving, an usher announces that Dr. Browne is waiting to consult with me in my presence chamber if I would receive him. I cock my head to the side, trying to recall if I summoned a doctor.

Lady Mathilda leans in to whisper, "Your husband thought you should see him. He heard you were ill."

Doing my best not to show my discomfort, I let my eyes sweep over her. A spy in my midst. I should have known my husband would monitor me. It's sweet he is concerned and sent for a doctor. What is leaves a bitter taste on my tongue is that he heard I was ill from someone else.

"Yes, of course. I shall join him shortly," I say to the waiting usher.

Dr. Browne sweeps me a deep bow and asks me to sit. He has brought a bag of his trade, full of potions and tinctures that promise to cure any ailment.

His voice is a soft timbre as he questions me about my

symptoms and feels my pulse. Then he speaks to my lady's maids.

I watch him nodding at their answers, and I'm desperate to know what he is asking them. If it is something serious I should know, shouldn't I?

At last he is done and he smiles as he mixes me a white cream.

"If you rub this on your back every morning, then you will find your pain eased."

"Thank you." I pause, waiting for him to say more. "And my sickness? It will go away?"

There's a twinkle in his eye as he says, "Yes, I imagine so. In a few months."

"A few months?" My brows furrow, but then I see the smiling faces of my ladies and the doctor's delighted expression and I guess what he will say before he says it. My hand drifts to my belly. "I am with child?"

"I suspect so. It will probably be another month before you will feel your child, if there is one, quicken. Shall I write to inform your husband, or do you wish to be the one to tell him the joyous news?"

Bile rises in my throat. A combination of happiness and fear. I suppress the emotion with a smile. "I shall tell him. Thank you, Dr. Browne."

He tilts his head and with another bow leaves.

My ladies all rush around me to congratulate me.

"You must not ride out anymore, my lady." Abigale reminds me more of my mother than a twenty-year-old unmarried woman.

"We cannot know for certain that I am with child.

But I will take care. However, I would prefer to avoid the embarrassment of being wrong. Please, all of you, say nothing to my lord husband. Swear it to me." My gaze travels from one person to another before settling on Mathilda. She is frozen in place, her lips pulled back in a grimace, but at last even she nods and swears. I pray she shall keep my secret. She has nothing to gain.

As I prepare to leave Penshurst Place, my mind is whirling. There's another secret reason for my desire for secrecy. What if, despite all my father's careful planning, the queen wishes to set this marriage aside? I would be little more than a harlot if I were unmarried and carrying a babe in my belly.

The thought that I might have a child to hold in my arms makes my throat dry. It feels too soon to leap from newlywed to mother. It's not a prospect I think of with revulsion, but I thought I might have more time.

But when did anyone listen to my opinion?

The queen is at her favourite palace, Richmond. The closer we get to London the more certain I am that I have crossed a veil into another world. There are so many people all crammed into one city. The scent of opportunity and excitement in the air as vendors jostle each other for the best spot to set up their wares. But equally it's hard to ignore the poverty in the hungry faces of beggars on the side of the road. I hand out alms as much as I can, but I cannot help everyone.

When we arrive and I emerge from the litter my ladies have forced me to ride in, I expect to find my husband waiting to greet me. Instead, it is Lord Burghley who has taken time out of his busy day to come bid me good day.

"It is a pleasure to see you, Lady Frances. The last time I saw you, you were missing your two front teeth."

I show him all the respect and deference his rank demands.

"That was a very long time ago." I force myself to smile and hide the quiver of my hand in my billowing sleeve. "I am surprised you remember."

"It has been. So much has changed." He pauses, searching my face. His every word and posture invites me to confide in him, but I pull back as if he has bared his teeth. I know his tactics. The fact that he is employing them now does not bode well for me.

The desire to ask where my husband is sits on the tip of my tongue, but I swallow it down. I will not speak without a measure of calculation.

"Are you here to take me to the queen? I would prefer to wash the dirt from the road off my face, but I also do not wish to keep her waiting."

His tender smile wavers before contorting into something that I can only describe as a devious grin. "I will take you to her majesty now. There's no sense in delaying."

He holds out his hand to me. A hunched-over youth in fine clothes shuffles behind him. Lord Burghley catches me looking at him.

"My son, Robert. He's my pride and joy. He shall stay and instruct your household where they may bring your things."

I nod and take his offered hand at last.

The palace is one of the queen's smaller homes, yet it is still breath-taking as we walk through the rich halls. No one interrupts us or even casts more than a perfunctory gaze at us as we stroll by.

This isn't meant to be a tour, but Lord Burghley stops occasionally to point something out. A tapestry. A painting. I find it hard to keep on high alert around him. We take back staircases and secret passages to reach the queen's presence hall. I am not given the chance to catch my breath and am simply pushed forward into the room.

Queen Elizabeth sits enthroned beneath the canopy of estate, her face in shadows as the sunlight pours through the windows behind her.

On her right stands Robert Dudley, Earl of Essex. This is my husband's uncle, but I know that his loyalty is to himself first. I search the faces in the crowd to see if Philip is here. He is not. Has he been arrested? That is a possibility. My father is also absent. He will have known by now that I have been commanded to come to London. It's probable that he already knows I am here. If everything goes wrong, surely he can rescue me.

I fix my gaze upon her majesty, falling into a deep obeisance as she studies me. There's something predatory about her. I've been pushed into the lion's den. She leans back and now I can make out her features. Her lips purse in displeasure, as if she did not drag here me but rather interrupted her.

I stay down, my eyes now fixed on the floor, ignoring my burning thighs as they strain from the effort. I do not let my weakness show and hope that my submissiveness is enough to earn some reprieve.

"You may come closer, Lady Frances. Let me get a good look at the face that has melted the heart of our court poet."

I can hear the sneer in her voice, but I obey. I have not had time to paint my face and I am not dressed in finery that would be fitting for a meeting with the queen. Then again, I am not here for pleasure. I am on trial. The queen's face is an unearthly white mask. From afar it looked like polished stone, but up close I can see the cracks. I am glad that I am not forced to be at court day in and day out. I would hate to cover my skin in the white lead that is so popular, no matter how elegant the effect is from afar.

I force myself to look away and watch her long fingers, famous for their skill with pen and lute, twitch beneath my contemplative gaze. There is a ring on every finger, and the jewels catch the light.

"Look into my face so I can see if you are telling the truth," the queen says. This time her command has less of a bite to it.

Anxiety that I might say or do the wrong thing prevents me from obeying her right away. Only when I remind myself that she is only a human woman do I finally vanquish my fear and make eye contact with her.

The queen bends forward. A cool hand under my chin moves my head from side to side.

"Hmm. Nothing spectacular. What do you say, Robert?"

I flush red with embarrassment at this examination.

"I would say you are tormenting this creature." The sound of his heels as he approaches echoes in the quiet hall, but I dare not look in his direction. "You know already there is none more beautiful than yourself, my queen."

The grip on my chin relaxes and then is gone.

The queen pulls away and she regards me with a piercing look.

"Tell me how is it you have married one of our most famous celebrities. I thought Philip Sidney would never marry. He swore he could love no one but me. I know that is nothing but a lie to soothe the ego of an old woman."

It would be easy to flatter her and deny the truth. I am ready to speak the words, but something stops me. I am not sure whether it is godly intervention or the strange glint in her eyes that alerts me, but I am thankful for my intuition that bids me down another path.

"You are timeless. What is one mere mortal man to yourself, Your Majesty? A marriage such as ours cannot hold a flame to the love and devotion he holds for you."

Her lips part as though in shock. Then she grins up at Robert Dudley, who is now in arm's reach of her.

"Dear Robin, take note. It's been a long time since you have spoken such sweet words to me." She turns back to me. Her expression has changed. Our queen is mercurial. Now that her features are relaxed and the dark cloud tainting her mood has lifted, I can see that she must have been a beautiful woman. That beauty has not faded but morphed into majesty and gravitas with age. She exudes power and the most frightening thing: control. I don't need to recall my father's stories about her to see that she knows how to wield it. "Lady Frances, you have married without my blessing. Do you regret it?"

Again I don't reply. My mind is whirring as I think of what to say. I cannot blame my father without putting him in danger. Nor can I lie and claim that this clandestine affair was of my own making. We are clearly not madly in love with each other. I remember my husband's words to me. The queen knows of our marriage. She is merely toying with me. But nothing is a surety. She is playing with the rings on her fingers, and I know I stand on the brink of destruction. My survival depends on what I say next.

"It would honour me to have it now." I fall into another deep curtsy at her feet. Prostrating myself before her. Harmless and innocent. My life is in her hands.

She blinks. "But you don't say that you would give anything for it."

"I have nothing that I could offer you." I fight on. The last thing I need is to talk myself into a corner. "I am nothing."

"Your father has done me a disservice by not allowing you to come to court. Or perhaps a favour. That remains to be seen." Once again the queen places her royal hands on my head. I do my best not to flinch away. "Lady Frances Sidney, you have my blessing for this union. May it prove fruitful. Look at me, girl."

I obey.

"You have married without permission. Regardless of whether or not it was by your doing." She pauses to let the words sink in. My heart is pounding rapidly in my chest. I know my eyes are wide with fear. "I know the world isn't kind to women. There are always men who would make pawns out of us. So just this once I extend mercy and forgiveness to you. I can see you are clever, so I know you will understand me when I say that I am not a woman who forgives easily or goes back on her word. Don't disappoint me again. You shall live to regret it if you do."

I swallow and bow my head so low that I could kiss her feet.

"You are gracious, Your Majesty."

"Was there any doubt?"

The hall fills with laughter.

Just like that I am dismissed. I cannot tell if Lord Burghley is disappointed as he leads me away from the room.

"You will want to rest," he says, snapping his fingers. "Young Essex here will escort you to your rooms."

A young man not much older than myself materialises at his side. His cap is askew and he is smoothing over the creases of his jacket. There is something about the way he looks at me that makes me think he is eager to snap me in two.

"Lady." He sweeps me a bow. "I would be honoured."

I stiffen but try not to let my discomfort show. Lord Burghley is already returning to the queen's side.

I walk in silence, ignoring Essex as he whistles a tune. He walks around the halls of Richmond Palace as though he owns them.

"You are far too serious, my lady. Don't you know you have accomplished an amazing victory? You should celebrate."

"What have I accomplished?" I cannot help but ask. His eyes search my face. He will not find any sign of deception there.

He cocks his head to the side, amused. "You have surprised the queen and outplayed her. She will not appreciate you for your cleverness, you know. She was hoping you would fall weeping at her feet."

"Then I have failed to please her," I say, keeping my voice cool.

"Far from it." Essex is conspiratorial as he leans in closer to whisper, "I think you have given her something she didn't even know she wanted. Thus you have won the ultimate game."

"You enjoy speaking in riddles, young master." I keep my back straight, pretending that I am not flattered by his words. I can see in his eyes the spark of admiration as he regards me. But I am far more irritated at him.

"You seem to know the queen well, and yet I have never heard of you before."

We reach a set of double doors. He grins. "Soon the

whole world shall know my name. I am playing a long game, but I plan to win."

"Your words are nonsense and spoken like a child. What game are you playing?" Ire at his arrogance rises within me.

"Your tongue has given me a good lashing, but I thought it was clear. We all play for the greatest prize: the queen's favour. It can bestow untold power. But I suppose you aren't interested."

The double doors open to reveal my husband.

My heart skips a beat at seeing him and a smile spreads across my face.

Essex has stepped away from me, bowing to Philip. "I have come to deposit your lady wife into your safe-keeping."

"Thank you." Philip's tone is impersonal. He motions me inside.

"Careful with that philanderer," he says, closing the door behind him.

I shrug. "He's harmless. Maybe arrogant, but I think he just wanted to rattle me. We have not seen each other in weeks. Why are we speaking of someone like him?"

He softens at last. "I know. I apologise. This has been a stressful week."

We are alone in his apartments. The servants have all been dismissed. I reach out and touch his face. "All is well. The queen has granted us her blessing."

His eyes alight on mine. "She has?"

"Yes," I say, stepping closer to him. I am happy to

have managed to get such a reaction from him. "And, dear husband, there is other news that should please you too." I am emboldened by my recent victory and step closer to him. He wraps his arms around me and I am not sure if it is to hold me away from him or as a sign of affection.

"Tell me."

"I believe I am with child. My courses have not returned and it's been three months since our wedding. The doctor suspected I might be. The one you so kindly sent."

He flushes but does not deny he has been spying on his own wife. Instead, he breaches the distance between us and places a chaste kiss on my forehead.

"You've done a good day's work and now you give me even further cause to be happy. Thank you."

I look into his eyes, searching for something more. I am disappointed to find him already pulling away from me.

"If you have a favour to ask of me, now is the time." He sits on a couch. "But first tell me everything that transpired in the queen's company."

I settle down across from him, ignoring the pangs in my heart, and try my best to recall everything that transpired.

He strokes his chin as he listens to my tale. "You have done well. I am impressed. Though a few tears might have pleased her even more."

He is joking, but I can see he is trying to puzzle me out. Had he been worried I would ruin everything?

"They would have been disingenuous. I have a feeling she would hate that above all else."

He nods. "You are right. How perceptive of you. I'm glad you thought quickly on your feet. You tread along the path of truth, reshaping it to suit our narrative. Well done."

I shift in my seat. I would be prouder of myself if this had been something I had planned all along. Or if my palms had not been sweating with anxiety as I stood before the queen. I want to leave London. I'm clearly not ready for its dangers. "And my father? Is he not here?"

"He was in a conference with the Scottish ambassador. But I am sure it will not be long before he hears of your arrival."

I am used to going for long periods of time without seeing my father. Throughout my childhood he was in and out of my life working on the queen's behalf. But this recent farewell, following my wedding, has felt different. I am no longer living underneath his roof and likely never will. A hand travels to my belly. Soon I might have a child of my own to care for.

My husband watches me from his seat. Something hungry in his eye. He looks as though he would reach out to me, but something is holding him back.

"You should rest. We are safe now. All of us."

His words strike home. Pure elation fills me. I can breathe easier knowing this child will be born Philip's acknowledged heir. For now we can be at ease that neither of us will be locked away.

My father is pleased to see me. He has already heard

of my success and tells me I have made him proud. I enjoy my short time in London before the weather grows hot.

There are whispers that this year the sweat will spread through England like wildfire. Without a word of warning, I find myself packed off to Penshurst Place. Everyone has been nothing but kind, but I cannot help but feel like a discarded piece of meat.

Beads of sweat travel from the nape of my neck down my back. There's no escape from the stifling heat and certainly not in the litter with the curtains pulled around me. We cannot take any chances with foul vapours, so we cannot open them to let fresh air in. Not that the air outside provides any respite. The retinue of guards escorting me are no better off than I am. There is no breeze or sign that there will be a break from this intolerable heat.

On the other hand, the dry warm weather has been good for the crops. As we travel, I can see the wheat in the field is growing tall. We might get two harvests this year.

The farther we get from London the more uneven the roads. The litter jostles me back and forth. My ladies do their best to help me as my hand drifts to my belly to steady myself. Despite my continued lack of appetite in the morning, my stomach is beginning to curve and I have to order the maids to loosen the ties of my gown. Soon I will put away the more fashionable dresses and lounge in robes of silk. When winter comes I will exchange those for furred gowns. On my fingers, I count out the months until the birth. I could be wrong but by all estimation I will present my husband with his child by the New Year. A part of me wishes that I knew exactly how much time I have left, but I hadn't been paying attention and the doctor and midwives cannot help me.

I suppose I shall know when my child is ready to come into the world. I am not a queen or duchess whose lying in will be watched and recorded with all the ceremony and pomp of a coronation. Courtiers will not wait outside my apartments, bribing the midwives for news of the birth. The child I carry in my womb is a blessing for our family rather than the whole nation. I am thankful for this.

Once we reach Penshurst Place I settle into the monotony of daily life. I take care to dry herbs that prevent the sweat and I direct the house to be aired out and cleaned more frequently. There is nothing like foul airs to invite disease into one's home.

I hear from my mother on a weekly basis. She is concerned for me alone in the country. The more instructions she gives me the less inclined I am to invite her to stay with me.

It's Lady Mary who arrives without my foreknowledge. She has fled her fabulous London home. I don't ask why she has come here, nor why she sequesters herself in my husband's rooms reading over documents.

But at last one morning after chapel I ask her how long she plans to stay at Penshurst.

"Philip asked me to come stay with you," she says, as if that were obvious. "He likes to get a detailed account of what goes on here, and that would be hard for me to do if I was all the way in London."

"Why doesn't he ask me for one?" I am too stunned by her revelation to hold back my surprise. "I would be happy to keep him abreast of all that goes on here."

She pats my cheek. "He doesn't want to trouble you. After all, aren't you still settling in? Enjoy yourself. This doesn't need to trouble you."

But it does trouble me. Countless possibilities gnaw away at my confidence.

Lady Mary is out riding in the woods when a delivery arrives from London. Three boxed crates are deposited on our doorstep. There is no note or instructions, so I instruct the men to deposit the boxes in the great hall.

I stand by as I watch them pry open the lids. Approaching with all the nervousness of a colt, I push away the straw padding to reveal freshly printed pamphlets beneath. Carefully, I pull one out. I can still smell the ink and paper.

I am surprised to find my husband's name on the cover. As I flip through the pages I can see that these are his pages. He has published his work and I knew nothing of it.

I stop at a sonnet named "Astrophel and Stella." It's beautiful. A love sonnet if there ever was one. Stella is the star that Astrophel is drawn to. He was born to love her.

"Ah, they are here." Lady Mary's voice interrupts my reading.

My eyes widen and I nearly drop the pamphlet as if I've been caught snooping.

She approaches and takes the pamphlet from my hand. She stares down at the passage I was reading, her brows furrowing as she regards me more carefully.

"Did he not tell you he was publishing some of his better-known works?"

Still struggling to find my voice, I shake my head. "Everyone called him a poet, but I never saw or read any of his work. Until now." I take a deep breath. Was this the reason he kept me at arm's length? This woman he writes such beautiful poetry too? I try my best to swallow this bitter pill.

"That is a shame. You may have this one then." She hands me back the pamphlet I had been reading. "Our father always thought we were foolish to waste our time on such flighty pursuits."

"I find that surprising."

"In a way he's not wrong." Mary lets out an exasperated sigh as she searches through the rest of the crates and then orders them to be stored in my husband's office. "Thinking of the danger we are in, we shouldn't waste time on literary pursuits. However, this is what feeds our soul. Don't you think so?"

I think of my love of reading and the myths from antiquities that have captured my mind. "I agree with you. We'd be no better than animals if all we did was fight and conquer."

"We artists are still waging a war to sway people's hearts. But I'm afraid we are losing. The more time goes on, the more devious we have become, but still we behave like wild beasts. You don't see duels anymore or chivalry on the field of battle. It's all gunfire and theatrics."

The passion in her voice sparks something within. I cannot help but lean toward her with rapt attention.

"My brother thinks as I do." She goes on, staring off into the distance. "That's why he admires the queen so much. She is averse to war and enjoys debate and scholarly pursuits as much as any professor at Cambridge. Not to mention her love of languages. Did you know she can speak over five fluently?"

I shake my head. Carefully, I don't tell her that I thought there was no language the queen didn't know. "I know she has a love of theatre too. She has always stood against those who would close the theatres."

"Yes. We should work on becoming an enlightened nation. Well, maybe it will be possible once this mess with the Scots queen is resolved and we will be able to focus on something other than the threat of war."

As if remembering where she is, Lady Mary turns to me, her face apologetic. "You must not let me exhaust you."

"No, I've enjoyed our conversation. I feel so ignorant about my own husband and I have no one else that could talk with me as you do."

She inclines her head in acknowledgment. "Well, you can get to know him quite well through these." She points to the pamphlet I am clutching to my stomacher.

"You are right. I shall study every word."

Her laugh is light and melodious as it travels around the room. "He's not that good of a poet. When you finish with that I shall send you some work from my personal collection. Might I recommend you don't worry about every little thing he writes."

My grip on his pamphlet tightens until I can feel the spine digging into my palm.

5

WINTER 1584 - SPRING 1587

I should have heard the warning in Lady Mary's advice when she told me not to analyse my husband's words. The poems wax and wane, pining for love so deep that even death cannot separate them.

Philip wrote the poems before our marriage. It would be ridiculous to even think he was writing about us. I wonder again about the way he pulls away from me, and though he shows me every respect and offers me untold comforts, he does not open his heart to me. I hardly even receive a letter from him, and often he shows up at Penshurst unannounced as he passes through to his other houses and goes about his business.

I wonder if he has a mistress tucked away somewhere. Were these poems about her? My pride is injured, but I am surprised to find that at last my heart has stopped aching for more than he can offer. If he were here, I would tell him I might not care if he has a hundred mistresses but I would prefer if he didn't write or publish such beautiful poetry about them.

The threat of the plague leaves with the cool autumn breeze. Our child is growing in my belly. I feel him kick ferociously in the evenings, preventing me from sleeping well. It's this little being growing inside me that has captured my love and attention. Lady Mary packs up her things and leaves me alone once more.

Managing our estate and preparing the nursery keeps me busy. A calmness fills me, or perhaps that is merely exhaustion cutting through the anxiety I feel. My father has warned Queen Elizabeth that her cousin is busy plotting something.

The queen has responded by restricting her movements further, which of course earned her a rebuke from the Spanish ambassador. The Spanish emperor pretends to come to Mary's defence, but really he is using her as an excuse to invade our nation. I don't think he's ever forgiven Elizabeth for refusing to marry him—even after all this time.

It's a shame that the squabbles of monarchs hurt their subjects so much. Spain threatens to cut off English merchants from trade thus, crippling our economy. This year the harvest has been good, but there were other years when we relied on imported wheat to fill our bellies. If the Spanish were to blockade the channel, then we would be left to starve. England has neither the allies nor the firepower to defeat them, but we pretend as if this is not true.

October brings lots of surprises to my doorstep. The first being my husband. He arrives in the dead of night with three trusted men at his side.

There is trouble. But why should that surprise me or anyone who works to keep the queen safe?

"Don't be frightened," Philip says. "I am on my way to Scotland, but if anyone has been tracking me I want them to think I have rushed back to you."

My eyebrow arches. "Would that be so ridiculous?"

He gives me a weary smile. "Wife, you know I would come if you beckoned me to your side."

"The poet emerges." I recline lazily on the divan. My legs are swollen. I am anything but attractive in this moment.

He approaches my side, taking my cool hand in his. "Do you have everything you need?"

"Of course," I say. "I lack for nothing. You have made me a great lady."

He catches the jest and reaches out a hand to my big belly. I see him hesitate just before making contact with it, so I take his hand in mine and place it firmly over the spot where I can feel our child kicking.

He jumps at the motion, and his eyes go wide with surprise. "Is that..."

"Your imp." I finish for him.

"Doesn't it hurt?"

"A little," I acknowledge. "But you get used to it. I think whoever is in here will be strong."

His eyes are warm pools as he bends down toward my belly until I can feel the hairs of his beard tickling my skin. “Be good for your mother and let her rest,” he whispers before placing a kiss in the spot where his hand had just been.

I could fall in love with him for this tenderness. When he looks up at me, my heart wrenches at the thought of what could have been.

On the desk near my bedside is his printed work. Stella stands between us. Whoever she was or is, she has his heart. I could ask him, but I’d rather never know.

“What has happened that has you riding to Scotland?”

He looks uneasy, as though he would rather not say. “Just work for the queen.”

“Does this have to do with the Scots queen again? Have there been any recent developments?”

Again he shakes his head. “I prefer you know nothing about this sordid business. But you are safe, don’t worry.”

I was young when the Duke of Norfolk raised an army and tried to march on London. The plan was to free Queen Mary and place her on the throne of England. He would marry her and they would rule together. That plan had been thwarted by the loyalty of Elizabeth’s subjects. But it could have just as easily ended in disaster. We live our lives on the edge of danger. It should terrify us, but I suppose after all this time we have grown used to it.

“Please remember whose daughter I am. If you are worried about my ability to keep a secret, I think I have proven myself by now. I hate being kept in the dark about such matters."

"Very well. Your father has discovered a plot. The Catholics are going to attempt another uprising. This time they are also trying to place her back on the Scottish throne. I am riding to obtain support from King James should they succeed in gathering an army."

I shake my head, not with incredulity but at the foolishness of the Scots queen. At this point it feels as though she is daring Elizabeth to act against her. My father has been pressing for her death for quite some time. He hates everything she represents.

My husband, guessing my thoughts, jumps ahead of me. "She isn't the threat she was ten years ago. Nor does she have the support she once did, but we must be prepared for every eventuality."

"I understand. Godspeed, husband."

He goes to his own room and rests for two hours before jumping on a fresh horse and heading north to the border.

~

By November the Throckmorton plot is unravelled. The conspirators are behind bars and even Queen Mary has been moved from being under house arrest to stricter imprisonment. Her household is reduced and she is no longer allowed to ride out. My father is working tirelessly to press our queen to bring her to trial.

We will never be safe while she is alive, but neither will we be safe after her death. It's simply that the danger will come from different quarters.

Philip's family gathers for a family party at Penshurst before he must return to court for the celebrations there.

I am now forced to waddle about, holding on to someone's arm for support. Seeing the size of me, the midwife suspects I am carrying twins. I pray that this is not the case.

As an early new year's gift Philip gives me a gold chain, an emerald brooch and a new cradle he had commissioned in London. It's decorated beautifully with finely carved leaves and painted angels. The gifts are generous and I am sure I will treasure them.

It's just after Christmas Day that I go into labour. My ladies shake the midwives from their beds and they come running to attend me.

The pains are coming faster and faster. I am panic-stricken, unable to keep a clear head or think rationally. All I know is that with each contraction I writhe on the bed they place me on as if I am eager to escape my own skin.

"Be calm, lady." The midwife checks my forehead for fever. She motions for one of my ladies to sponge my forehead with cool water. "You have a way to go before your baby is born. Take heart."

It's hard to be brave in the face of such uncertainty. I feel as though my body has betrayed me. They keep me talking until well into the morning. Mathilda reads to me

Cicero and Plato and either I become used to the pain or this distracts me long enough for me to relax.

The midwife plies me with strong birthing ale. The strong herbs and scent nearly make me retch, but then I settle into a stupor.

My daughter arrives just after noon, hollering for a feed. As suspected, she is a strong fighter. I take her to my breast, though I should pass her off to the waiting wet nurse.

The midwife exclaims over the size of her. "If you kept her in your belly any longer she would've come out walking and talking."

The room that had been filled with my wailing cries now fills with laughter.

The next day I write to Philip myself. I hope he will not be disappointed that our first child is a girl, but I already know he is too honourable to feel anything but joy.

The name of our daughter was already decided before her birth. We are to call her Elizabeth. My parents send their love along with a purse filled with gold and a christening gown for her. The queen surprises us by standing in as a godmother. It is a great honour and with it comes a set of pearls.

Congratulations flow in from all quarters, which I attribute to the popularity of my husband. We cannot have a grand christening for her because the queen, in a show of favour, has named Philip General of the Horse and is planning on sending him overseas as a commander in her army as war with Spain keeps threatening to break out.

He comes to give our child his blessing and stays long enough to see me churched. I can see how busy and distracted he is. Our world is expanding. The future is filled with limitless possibilities.

I only pray we don't break.

~

Winter's hold over England breaks and I pack up Elizabeth and a small retinue to visit my parents' house.

For once my father is home. He has been recovering from a terrible fever that made my mother fear for his life. They both marvel at the grandchild I have given them and remark that I look well.

"Boys will come," my mother whispers to me one evening. We are sitting by the fire watching Elizabeth squirm in her crib, free of the swaddling bands.

I want to point out that she only ever had me, but I can forgive her. This is just what people say on occasions such as these.

Little Lizzy's smile turns into a little frown and she cries. I reach for her and put her to my breast. I notice the frown on my mother's face.

"Don't you have a nursemaid to feed her?" she says.

Everyone disapproves, but I don't care what they think. I treasure her too much to let her go now.

"My husband says I may," I argue back. "Besides, he has not been home very often for us to think of another child." It's true. Since I was churched he has not come to my bed. This is partly because business with the queen keeps him so occupied but also because he has been sitting in parliament and helping my father. It's likely neither of us has much appetite for anything other than sleep.

"Well, as long as he approves. But you know people will talk. Your husband is rising higher in the queen's favour. Who knows, she might make him an earl."

I shrug, but really I'm just being stubborn. Of course the thought of an earldom thrills me, but around my mother I resume my childish behaviour.

Lady Anne Forrester enters the room. These days it seems like her eyes are always wet with tears. She claims it is nothing but another maid confides in me that a growth is pressing on her spine causing her terrible pain.

Her smile is genuine as she regards the three of us.

"Her ladyship is hungry, I see. Shall I summon the nursemaid to come look after her after she is done?"

I give a nod. Soon it will be time for my own dinner.

We sit around a small table. This is a private meal just for the family. My father is muttering something under his breath as he watches the manservant carve a joint of smoked venison.

He dismisses him as soon as he is done.

"I've hired a bunch of lazy rascals."

"They are nothing of the sort." Knowing my mother will never contradict him, I rush to defend my father's servants. "Not everyone can work as hard as you do. Not that I would advise anyone to do so, given how you've nearly worked yourself into an early grave."

"Frances," my mother hisses at me.

I watch my father, whose eyes darken before his grimace breaks into a chuckle. "My brave little lion cub has sharpened her claws while she was away from us."

"What has put you in such a dark mood?" I am conciliatory to him now.

He regards me with a look as if he's weighing the scales. I understand his conundrum. A good spymaster is always afraid of revealing his thoughts and even more so his secrets.

At last he leans back in his seat.

"The Scots queen has been busy."

My breath catches in my throat. So soon? Her last plot was just uncovered. Many people died trying to help her. Why would she dare try again?

"Will she never give up?" I close my eyes and not for the first time wish death upon someone I've never even met. All the threats to our realm stem from that woman. If only she were gone.

"No. She will not. Just as I or our queen would never stop." He clicks his tongue impatiently.

"Why can some accident not befall her?"

"You know well why not."

Of course I do, but it doesn't make it any easier. I want to go see my child. I don't want to talk of politics and intrigues that could see all of England fall under Spanish rule. My family, strong Protestant defenders, would be brought before the Spanish inquisition. I shake my head clear of the horrors that would befall us. We will not lose.

"I will order her kept so strictly not even a speck of dust will pass by without me knowing about it." My father is pensive. Queen Mary has always been his greatest challenge.

My mother reaches out for him. I watch her take his hand in hers and stroke the back of it in slow soothing strokes. A thought strikes me.

"You could try, but one day sooner or later she will find a gap."

He hates I am right so he doesn't argue, but his eyes narrow. "So what shall I do?"

He wants to teach me a lesson. To humble me. I look at the half-eaten food on my plate as I try to rack my brain, thinking of a solution. It's intimidating to think that my father, the cleverest of men, has not thought of a solution. I can hear the tapping of his fingernails as he waits for my reply. Unbidden stories of nymphs and dryads, ogres and vengeful monsters fill my head. I curse myself for thinking of such things at such a time. Then I go still as an answer falls into my lap. I could laugh.

"Well?"

I glance up, meeting his gaze confidently. He is taken aback by this and arches a brow. "If she will eventually find a gap, why not be the one to provide it?"

He releases a breath. His eyes gleam with excitement as he considers what I have said. A hand strokes his long pointed beard and he inclines his head to me.

"That could indeed be the answer. It will have to be

managed carefully. She's not a fool. Many have underestimated her before."

My mother is still stroking his hand. "You wouldn't fail."

He pulls away from her. "It would be a sin to think so. Overconfidence in this matter will be our downfall. She has been within my grasp for years now and yet she always avoids the noose and traps laid out for her. Once or twice could have been attributed to happenstance, but she's a dangerous player in her own right."

He turns to me. "You have shown me how blinded I can be by my own conceit. I apologise for underestimating you."

I straighten at his words. My heart is overwhelmed by joy at his acknowledgment.

We don't speak of the Queen of Scots again. Once my father returns to London, I leave for Penshurst Place.

On our journey back I marvel at Elizabeth's growth. She can now sit up on her own and is eager to chew anything she can sink her gums into.

Life falls back into the predictable pattern dictated by the seasons and the church.

To my relief, Elizabeth survives smallpox though it claims the lives of three people and a child in the nearby village. My husband sees us infrequently, and though he suggests he might set us up in a London house, I tell him I prefer being in Kent.

A year passes us by. I have held on to Elizabeth as she takes her first steps and taught her how to speak a few words here and there. She occupies my time, but I do not slack in my care of our lands. I operate my household with efficiency, and I don't let our suppliers swindle us just because we are gentry. Most would be too proud to haggle with the fishmonger, but I have no misgivings. However, I never forget to be as generous as our income will allow. I cannot stand to see people go hungry and set up a hospital that might provide food and work for those in need. It's an expense, but it buys us the love and loyalty of our tenants. Now there's no excuse for ruffians that are found harassing and thieving in the hamlets and villages nearby. I ensure the sheriff sees justice done.

As I attempt to hide away in the country and pretend the affairs of Europe and greater people than myself don't affect me, rumours of unrest reach me. My father writes to instruct me to buy up steel and stockpile gunpowder while prices are still reasonable. I go a step further and expand the forge.

At night I dream of blood, and in the morning I wake with the taste of metal in my mouth.

Elizabeth is too young to know what is going on, but she is thrilled when her father arrives bearing gifts. She loses her shyness of him from the moment he tickles her cheeks and picks her up. After that they are inseparable as he walks around our home looking over the provisions I have made.

"I am surprised to find you have not fortified our home. I was expecting to scale walls just to get in."

I grin. "If I could find the stone and the funds for it, I would be happy to oblige. My dream would be to go underground and hide until I am sure we are safe."

His hand is at my waist, and he pulls me toward him in an embrace that is meant to be comforting but feels stifling. "The queen has signed a treaty with the Netherlands. We will help them fight the Spanish, and thus we hope to weaken their hold in Europe and free our Protestant brethren."

My heart pounds in my chest. "And you are going?"

"Robert Dudley will lead her armies..."

"You are avoiding my question." I don't care that I have interrupted him. I shift in his arms, trying to get free.

He releases me, his dark eyes studying mine. Philip understands I will not be distracted.

"Very well, yes. The queen has given me the honour of leading troops alongside my uncle, the Earl of Leicester, and Sir John Norris."

"Surely my father can speak for you. The queen will listen to him. You don't need to go."

He chuckles and I feel like a fool. "Your father is the one who suggested I go. He wants me to keep an eye on both Essex and Leicester. They are both eager to prove themselves on the battlefield, but we fear what will happen if the power goes to their heads."

Now it's my turn to laugh. "What do you think will happen? Do you think they'd be foolish enough to ride back to England with an army at their heels and depose the queen? They both love her."

"And she keeps them at bay." I watch his eyes fix on the tapestry depicting a hunt that covers the wall of my presence chamber. It was a gift from his father. "Power corrupts the best of us, Frances. If they begin to stray, I will be there to stop them."

"You?" My hand drifts to my chest. I cannot imagine my husband turning on his general.

"I will do what honour dictates. For the good of my country. I will protect the queen."

I remember the cracked porcelain veneer. How she exuded power. Robert Dudley was hers to command. They all were.

"But there is something that might interest you. I once promised you that if I was sent away overseas I would not abandon you to wait for me in England. So tell me, what do you say to that?"

"I could not take Elizabeth into danger," I say without hesitation. "But I will come with you for a time if you think it is safe."

"You will be garrisoned deep in friendly territory. None shall harm you, but it will be nice to know I have a friendly face to ride home to every night."

I incline my head at the compliment. "It's settled then. We are off on an adventure."

His smile is strained. "God willing we will be successful."

My home in the Netherlands is humble compared to Penshurst Place, but I do not complain. The treacherous journey across the sea was enough for me to be thankful for solid ground.

I have two maids to attend to me, and though I have to sometimes stoke the fire myself and mend my own stockings, I am happy and filled with purpose. For the first time my work truly matters. So I pour my time and energy into keeping up with Philip's correspondence both back in England and here. There's never a shortage of work to be done, and Philip would rather trust me than some wayward clerk that can be bought for a few shillings to spill secrets to the Spanish.

I thought I was heading into danger, but I fear the news back in England is worse. Another plot to assassinate the queen has been stopped. I don't know if my father knew of Babington's plots and arrested him in the nick of time or if it was Anthony Babington's loose tongue that proved to be his undoing. Reports say he had been drunk the night before the assassination was to take place and began telling everyone who would listen that soon the true queen would sit on the English throne. He had worked with the Spanish ambassador to send missives between him and Mary. This is just the sort of ammunition Cecil and my father would need to entrap Mary. But I am just as unsurprised that the queen still hesitates to act.

I am never short for company. The mayor of the city and his wife always invite me to dine with them, and I am introduced to all the notable people. Most can speak

English decently well, and I do my best to pick up as much of their language as I can. Some know Latin or French, so we communicate using a patchwork of languages. They are kind and welcoming. When possible, Leicester and Essex both come to dine at our house. I am glad to see familiar faces but uneasy around these suave courtiers.

Usually I wait every night for news of my husband and pray he is safe and returns to me.

In September he leaves to join Sir John Norris in battle. He doesn't tell me much, but I can tell from his strained face that the war is not going well. The Spanish are better provisioned and have more men.

I place my hands over his head and give him my blessing before he takes me in his arms and kisses me. I smell his familiar scent and take that moment to whisper to him that I have missed my courses.

His hand drifts down to my belly and he kisses me again.

The next time I see my husband he is surrounded by doctors and white with pain. A bullet is lodged in his leg. If he survives the infection, he will never walk again without a cane. They tell me how brave he was. How he refused water offered to him on the battlefield but gave it to a fellow solider in much more dire need than himself.

That is my husband: the honourable man.

I am at his side night and day, sponging his forehead as the infection takes hold and the fever makes him delirious.

Sometimes he is lucid enough and he speaks to me.

He tells me of his childhood and the plans he envisioned for our family. Once he cries.

"What is wrong?" I am at his side in a moment, imagining he is weeping from some new pain.

But he merely laughs. "Frances, I forgot."

"Forgot what?"

"To take you to the theatre. I promised I would and I have failed you. Then again, I thought there would be more time," he says, then winces in pain.

I give his hand a squeeze. "Don't be foolish. You will get better. Think of all the things you have to do. Your children need you. The country does too."

"And you?"

I cannot help but be insolent. "I shall manage."

He laughs. "You deserve a better husband."

I don't know what to say, but he slips back into sleep a moment later.

I write to my parents, but I don't know if the letter will reach them in time. Philip has distinguished himself on the battlefield. He was a fearless commander and unparalleled strategist. If we had more men and supplies, then nothing would have stood in his way.

Leicester comes to his bedside. His uncle is in shock that he should see the nephew who was such a rising star in the world fall so far. I watch from afar as the men converse. I try not to think about the fact that my husband was prepared to kill him if he betrayed the queen.

When he turns to me with tears in his eyes, my chest tightens. I can tell he loved Philip. "Lady Frances, I will pray he shall recover. God will surely not let him leave us so soon."

I bite my tongue to stop myself from sobbing.

Sickness keeps me away when Essex comes to pay a visit. I am throwing up the little that I have forced myself to eat. He is getting ready to leave just as I am entering the room.

Essex bows his head in greeting but cannot seem to find the words to speak to me. We stare at each other, and I see my own deadpan expression reflected in his.

"Frances," my husband calls out, breaking the spell. I rush to his side and Essex disappears.

"Yes, dearest," I coo to him. "Can I get you anything?"

"M-my sword." His voice is weak and he struggles to form the words.

"Yes?"

"Make sure Essex g-gets it."

"Are you sure?" I frown, but then I realise what he's saying. "You must stop speaking like this. Remember, you cannot die. I order you to live."

He gives me a weary smile and fresh tears spring to my eyes, which by now are red and raw.

Day by day my husband grows weaker. The further he drifts away from life, the more secrets he spews forth. Often he calls out for Penelope, which I now think is the name of his love. When I am at his side comforting him, he searches my face with delirious eyes and I can tell he is disappointed I am not her. It hurts but I know he is in far greater pain.

Then one day he is gone. His body will be embalmed and encased in a lead coffin so they can transport it back to England for the hero's funeral that awaits him. With his last breath, he said her name. I hide the truth from the officials and instead claim he was incoherent to the last. They will spin their own story. But perhaps, as in all things, the truth does not matter. Already there are legends spread about his glorious deeds on the battlefield. I predict they will embellish the truth further, but at least I know that at the heart of it is truth: he was a good man.

Meanwhile, I have been cast adrift: a widow without friends or family nearby. I feel too young for the sorrow that seeps into my bones. I am not well, and I fear for the child growing in my womb just as I despair at the sudden loss of the life I had envisioned for myself.

It will be a long time before I can return home to my daughter. So I spend my days making bandages and stitching banners for the English army.

When news reaches us that the unthinkable has happened and that the Queen of Scots was beheaded, we brush it aside as mere rumour. Queen Elizabeth has put it off for so long no one on this side of the sea gives it any countenance. But then an official decree is issued and it is confirmed: Mary Stuart, the former queen of France and Scotland, is finally dead. I wonder if my father can sleep easier at night knowing that she is no longer plotting to take the throne.

Before my ship leaves port, I lose the child.

No one knows what to say to me anymore and I

board the ship without looking back at the land where I experienced so much misery.

I think of my daughter every night as the ship rocks me to sleep in my cabin. Memories of her dimpled smile remind me that not all is lost. I must set aside despair. Life will begin anew.

6

WINTER 1587 - SUMMER 1588

My father is waiting for me at the dock. As I step off the gangplank I notice he has grown thin as a rod and his skin is sallow.

"Daughter, I am glad to see you safe."

He escorts me back to Scadbury Hall. There is no question of me going to Penshurst Place all on my own. My husband's estate will be divided up and portioned out to his heirs. If my husband had inherited the wealth and title from his father, then my daughter would have been his heir. As it stands now, it is Philip's younger brother that will inherit. At least I will have my widow's jointure, and I cannot imagine that my father-in-law would let Elizabeth, who he dotes on, not have a proper dowry.

We speak about finances on the way in order to avoid talking about harder things such as losing Philip Sidney.

My father doesn't approve of Leicester or Essex. He will scour the kingdom for another heir, someone that can take up the mantle and protect the queen when he is gone.

I look at him and cannot imagine him not being here, but life can be unpredictable and cruel.

Over the next few weeks my father prepares a grand funeral for my husband. It's a public relations exercise but also the expectations for a great English hero. The queen has given her consent for him to be interred at St. Paul's Cathedral with great fanfare. My father's coffers are emptied to give Philip the honour he deserves.

Of course I cannot attend, so perhaps that is why I begrudge them this exaggerated show of mourning. It tastes false on my tongue. He will be mourned, but why must we now be paupers?

Once the lawyers finish with his estate, I discover I am to be paid out the generous sum of three hundred pounds annually. My daughter will have two thousand for her dowry when it comes time for her to marry. The sword my husband cherished with the bejewelled handle goes to Essex, and I cannot stop myself from calculating what the ruby at the hilt could have bought us.

Despite my annuity, I can no longer afford to live on my own. My other option is to embark on another marriage; however, no one will think of marrying me for three hundred pounds when there are other heiresses with more. I don't think I have it in me to embark on a marriage so soon either. In the end, I am forced to move back to Scadbury Hall and rely on the kindness of my parents.

There is little women can do to alter their fates.

At least Lizzy brings joy to my days.

By spring my father has recovered his spirits and his old passion for plotting returns. Even I am to be put into play. There is no question of me going to court, but my father arranges for me to be a guest at North Hall, where the queen will stay for a few weeks as the guest of the Earl and Countess of Warwick.

I am here to act as my father's eyes and ears. After the Scottish queen's execution, the factions at court have been uneasy. The queen was upset and the Spanish are busy sharpening their swords. War is coming and fear is making everyone turn on each other. Of these two factions, Raleigh, the great explorer, and Essex are butting heads like bulls in the field vying for the queen's favour. Their attempts to discredit each other are merely separating the court and distracting everyone from their true enemy. My father, though supportive of Essex, finds him immature and unpredictable. None of these are ideal characteristics in an ally. He must pray that Leicester returns from military duty soon. However, even Leicester is being eclipsed by his stepson, Essex. The queen, though aging herself, prefers to surround herself with youth and vigorous individuals.

North Hall is a well-stocked house with a large deer park nearby. The change of scenery is a pleasant respite from Scadbury Hall.

I enjoy moving in different circles, and with the

queen's imminent arrival there is always something to do. Among my new acquaintances is Dorothy, who is Essex's sister. Being similar in age and disposition, we gravitate to each other and often sequester ourselves away from the group of noble ladies fussing over every little thing.

"I wrote to my brother to ask if the queen is aware of my presence here," Dorothy says to me as we walk through the gardens one day.

There's a whole team of hedge trimmers moving along behind us. The sound of their scissors clipping away at the greenery fills the silence.

"She still has not forgiven your marriage?" Like me, Dorothy committed the cardinal sin of marrying without permission. However, unlike me, she had the misfortune of marrying someone that the queen distrusted.

Dorothy shrugs. "On the surface perhaps she has. But she has not rescinded my exile from court."

I remember that, unlike me, Dorothy was among the queen's maids of honour. "Do you miss it?" My question is genuine, though I hope it doesn't cause her pain.

A curt nod from Dorothy tells me everything I need to know.

"It can be dull, but there were so many people to see and talk to. There's a sense of anticipation and of being there to be a witness to history being written."

I hide a shudder at the thought of being there when the queen went into a rage after news was brought to her that her cousin was executed, as if she had not ordered it. But it would be impolite to point this out, so instead I settle on a half-truth. "It sounds exciting."

We step off the path and sit on a bench beneath grape vines growing on the trellis.

"And what of you? I am surprised you have not begged your father for a position at court. Or was the queen so displeased with your marriage as well that she would not have you?"

I am used to Dorothy's forward way of speaking. But she often forgets the differences in our upbringing. My family was nothing while hers were always gentry and part of the court. Her grandfather was a courtier at King Henry VIII's court, and her grandmother was his bastard child. She has royal blood in her veins. Even though it is unacknowledged, it has always given her a certain status I will always lack.

"I suppose I might end up there one day. But for now my father prefers me to stay away from court. Even after I was married I didn't travel to court."

Dorothy nods. "The queen doesn't like her courtiers having their wives around. I doubt it has anything to do with your charms."

I smile as if I am comforted by this. We sit in the shade, enjoying the scent of fresh pine that permeates the air. It's a crisp day and we are neither too hot nor cold. It would be a shame to return indoors, but soon duty prompts us to get up and return to the mistress of the house.

~

A lookout warns us of the queen's arrival. He has spotted dust clouds on the horizon and we have had advanced warning from her messenger. We have waited for many hours in anticipation of this event.

Some women quickly run off to powder their faces again. We are all dressed in our best, but none of us would dare try to outshine the queen. Treading the path between extravagance and dowdiness is a difficult thing to manage, especially when some of the ladies are young and fair, their skin free of blemishes, while we know the queen is over fifty and her extensive use of face powders has made her pockmarks more evident.

We will all try to pretend she is our immortal ageless queen. Our greatest fear is disappointing her, for her wrath is terrible.

Though I am not among the prominent members of the household that greet the queen, I have a good vantage point and I can see her riding on her horse. Despite her age she refuses to ride in a litter, so instead she sits rigid and tall in the saddle, her face a mask of cool calculation.

Essex follows closely behind her. Even dirty and tired from the road he looks handsome as he flicks the reins to the groom and in one gracious leap he is off his horse. I watch him approach the queen, hand outstretched as though he would pluck her from the saddle himself.

"He's been made Master of the Horse," Dorothy informs me under her breath. She is proud, as any sibling might be.

My attention is drawn away from this courtly display of love to Raleigh's grim face. As if sensing his foul mood, his horse becomes agitated, forcing Raleigh to pull back on the reins.

Now that she is off her horse, we all bow to the queen until she commands us to rise. She greets her host and hostess graciously, but I catch her sweeping a glance over the waiting crowd, taking account of who is here and who is not. For the briefest of moments her eyes rest on Dorothy, who is standing off to my right, half-hidden by Lady Margaret in front of her. I freeze, wondering if the queen will be outraged by her presence or if Dorothy was right in assuming she doesn't care anymore. She is confident that her brother will smooth over any difficulty and that it won't be long before she is forgiven and back at court.

~

If the queen were so easy to predict, then she wouldn't have survived this long.

I am watching the Countess of Warwick tremble before her silent rage.

"I don't want her in my sight. It's bad enough she has been in my presence already."

"What shall I do, Your Grace?"

"Lock her in her rooms if you have to. I don't want to see her while I am here."

"Of course." The countess is doing her best to stop herself from shaking, but the way she grips her hands together shows how hopeless it is.

"And you, what are you doing here?" The queen's eyes snap to me.

"I was told to bring fresh towels to your rooms, Your Grace." Keeping my eyes downcast, I say a silent prayer. I am not lying, but I didn't have to dawdle to overhear this exchange.

I hear the click of her tongue. "I am tired," the queen announces.

Both the countess and I press ourselves against either end of the gallery, the wood panelling digging into our backs as the queen glides past.

We make eye contact for the briefest of moments and then we recover and move into action. After I deliver the towels, I am filled with pity at the thought of Dorothy being kept locked away. She had been so full of hope that this visit would see her returned to favour. Then again, it might not be too late.

Finding Essex is much easier than I would have thought. He is in the hall, playing cards with the men, but rather than pay attention he is busy recalling a feat of bravery on the battlefield. I watch him from the doorway, a sour taste in my mouth. Philip would never have boasted like this. It is unbecoming rather than heroic. The men playing with him lean forward as if amazed, but I can see one peek at Essex's hand while another slides a coin off the table.

Filled with disgust, I begin my approach. The men go quiet as they see me. Essex leaves his cards on the table to bow to me and kiss my hand.

"It has been too long, Lady Frances." His voice is a deep slow drawl. "How may I help you?"

I can smell the wine on his breath. He sounds as if he's attempting to seduce me. Hardly proper, considering I'm his cousin's widow. "Your sister needs you."

He sobers immediately. "You will pardon me, gentlemen," he says to his friends. "Family business calls me away."

He is pulling me away out of the hall and into the privacy of the corridor outside.

"I think you disapprove of me, my lady," he says.

At least he is perceptive. I don't deny it and merely shrug. "I find playing cards frivolous when we are on the brink of war."

"England is always on the brink of war. Besides, it helps me make friends."

I scoff and he nods. "True. They aren't the reliable sort, but I earn their support by little more than letting them pocket some money off of me."

He must see my incredulity, for his smile deepens. "Ah, you thought I didn't notice Herbert take that coin. Well, I am a consummate actor. But enough of this, what has happened?" His blue eyes have lost all sense of their easy-going frivolity.

I clear my throat. "The queen has ordered your sister to be confined to her rooms for the duration of her visit."

His eyes have become steel as he lets out a low hiss.

"I will speak to her. This is an insult to my family."

I am not sure who he means to speak to, but I'm not sure I want to stick around to find out. Instead, I flee back to the Countess of Warwick's rooms, afraid I have made matters worse.

Not a moment later we hear raised voices. We all freeze until the countess orders one of her ladies to sing a song and starts doling out tasks for everyone.

The next day, huddled together trying to make the most of the morning light, we have needlework on our laps. None of us are bothering to work. Instead, we exchange everything we know about what transpired the night before.

Essex demanded the queen apologise for embarrassing his sister like this. The queen refused. Somehow Raleigh had been involved and this only fuelled Essex's anger more.

He sent Dorothy away to one of his houses with a retinue of his guards. Then this morning he was gone. He has taken his horse and is riding for the port to take ship and return to fight in the Netherlands.

I can't believe the tale they spin before me. Surely this must be a lie. Or an exaggeration at least. My name is not brought up and I am grateful for this. The last thing I need is to be dragged into the court gossip and attract the ire of the queen.

It is a tense day of waiting. Eventually, out of boredom we get to work on embroidery and other little projects we have. The queen has closeted herself in her rooms. Only a few councillors go in and out, as the business of the kingdom cannot stop.

By evening, Essex is back. He is standing at the queen's side as some jugglers perform for us.

Their anger is spent and now they are merely content to be back in each other's company. We watch with frozen anticipation until late into the night when we retire to our beds.

The argument is to be forgotten. That much is clear.

But I cannot forget as easily as the rest of the court does. My head throbs as I try to puzzle out this childish behaviour. I hate the court and its childish games.

~

My father is pleased with me, but when he mentions he might ask the queen for a place for me at court I beg him not to.

"I want to stay here with Elizabeth," I say. "I am not meant for the court."

He raises his eyebrows incredulously. "You've made a quick study of it. I am sure you have nothing to fear."

I am insistent. "For little jaunts yes, however, I would work myself into exhaustion and die of stress before the day is out if you force me to live there."

He takes my hand in his. "I will not force you, daughter. Besides, it might be safer for you here in the country this summer anyway."

"What do you mean?" The lines on his face deepen as his eyes darken and lips narrow.

I hazard a guess. "War?"

A curt nod is my confirmation. "They might not come," I try to say, but he shakes his head.

"It's all but a certainty. Only God can stop them now."

"It's good I know some Spanish then." My jest falls on deaf ears.

"Take care of your mother. I shall be in London most days. Any message I send to you will be in code in case our letters get intercepted. I might even ask you to flee to Scotland."

"You wish us to flee?" I am flabbergasted.

He has a far-off look on his face. "The Spanish would seek their revenge upon me by hurting my family. They would send you for questioning by the inquisition and you would likely be burned for what they perceive as heresy."

My right hand travels up the length of my left arm as if to put out flames there. "Then I will flee as you bid me."

He kisses my forehead in blessing and is gone.

My dreams are filled with fire and death. I wake in the morning and think I taste ash in my mouth. I leap out of bed to find that the fire in my grate has gone out. A window has flown open and the strong wind is kicking up ashes around the room.

A closer look at the window tells me that the latch has broken. I do my best to close the window and look at the mess with an exasperated sigh.

The expenses of my husband's funeral have taken their toll on my father's already strained finances. The household staff has been reduced. Judging from my fireplace, it's been a few days since it last received a proper cleaning.

I am not too proud to roll up my sleeves and clean it myself, but first I have to find a broom and bucket.

Despite my father's assurances that the Spanish are coming, April passes us by and no word reaches us. The signs are all there. We hear the pope has sanctioned this war against us. The queen is doing her best to fortify the fortresses along the coast. She has ordered cannons and provisions to be prepared. My father has set up watchmen all along our coast, so at the first sight of Spanish ships we will have warning.

The armada has set sail, but we don't hear of the fleet in May or in June. Maybe it will never come.

Everyone is united against this foreign threat. Fear gnaws at us, but we push forward, gathering our weapons as we prepare to go down fighting if we have to.

I am in the garden with Elizabeth, watching her toddle from flower to flower trying to name the colours she sees, when the sound of bells pealing reaches us.

A shiver travels through me before the fear makes my heart pound in my chest.

Quickly, I scoop up Elizabeth in my arms and run inside. My mother is frantic as she runs to and fro like a chicken that has just lost its head.

"What has happened?" I ask, even though I know the answer.

"They have been spotted off the coast of Cornwall."

The English fleet is in Plymouth. Elizabeth squirms in my arms, wanting to get free. She doesn't understand why I have taken her away from her games. Her nursemaid comes forth and takes her from me.

"Don't leave the house," I say, as if the Spanish are already marching toward us.

"I won't, my lady," the nursemaid promises.

My mother has fallen into a chair. Sobs rack her body. I am at her side, rubbing her back in slow soothing circles. Marta runs to the kitchens to fetch some ale.

"Don't worry, Lady Mother. All will be well." I speak to her as if she might be Elizabeth, but her sobs don't abate.

"Your father is ill. His heart cannot take this."

"He won't be riding into battle," I try to assure her, but my mother is inconsolable. I suppose she thought the Spanish were making empty threats.

A letter arrives from my father saying that we are to arm and send as many men as possible to Tilbury. He suggests we garrison ourselves at his London house. London is a big city, and my father has plenty of friends that would give us refuge until we can escape England if it comes to it. Out here in the country we have neither walls nor men to defend us.

With all haste we manage to get ourselves to London. The streets are eerily quiet, save for the sound of the forges and blacksmiths pounding metal into weapons or plate armour.

At the market when I go to buy fish I see just as many

peddlers offering charms for protection as I do vendors of weapons. I frown at such superstition. These people will make a tidy profit off the fears of others with no regard for how they imperil their immortal soul.

Essex has been charged with guarding the Thames from an incursion upriver.

He passes through London and dines with the London mayor. I am there, at the behest of my father. With me I bring a message to give to him and a purse of coin he will need to buy the loyalty of his men. It is crucial we remain steadfast in the face of this enemy.

He catches my eye as he walks to the centre of the table. As the guest of honour, he will sit centre stage whereas I am regulated to the back.

We eat well and then the conversation starts up. We curse the Spanish, laugh at their foolishness for trying to invade us, and boast about the prowess of our soldiers. It's a facade. Underneath we are all praying that a miracle will take place.

In the midst of all of this the lord mayor calls for music and dancing to lighten our moods. It's during this time that Essex makes his way to me. I notice him approaching out of the corner of my eye.

He bows to me and looks expectant. We cannot waste time on frivolity. The last thing I would want is some rumour spreading. I pass him the sealed letter and nod to him.

"I am glad to see you are in better spirits, my lady." He says, "Don't trouble yourself over something as small as the Spanish. I shall get vengeance for you."

He waxes poetic, but I hear the emptiness in his voice. Almost as if he's being sarcastic. Looking at him more closely, I can see that he has changed since I last saw him at North Hall. He is far more grave and serious. Then again, there was always more to him than meets the eye. Behind that veneer of a polished gentleman is a cunning calculating man.

I nod. The pain of losing my husband has dulled into a blunt blade. It is only at night that I struggle to fall asleep without seeing his lifeless face.

"Take care, Lady Frances." His farewell is a whisper and I follow his progress onto the dance floor.

He is light and graceful on his feet. I can see why the queen has made him her favourite. But I believe my father is right. He is unpredictable and hot-tempered.

As the dancing has begun in earnest now, I excuse myself and retire for the night. Being widowed so recently it would be impolite if I joined the fray.

News grows unreliable and anything we hear is contradicted soon after.

Essex has ridden out to Tilbury with the queen and Leicester where the English army is garrisoned. We hope it will not come to a battle on land, but even if they outnumber us at least we will know the terrain better than our enemies.

Then in August we hear that the Spanish armada has

been scattered by terrible winds while the English vessels have remained safe.

Fireworks and bonfires are lit in the streets. Men and women dance around like wild animals, cheering and calling out their thanks to God and England's queen.

For the first time in ages I sleep without dreaming of my husband's death. Even if this is the first of many battles, at least we have shown we are a force to be reckoned with.

The queen has returned to Greenwich. There is a great air of anticipation and excitement as news spreads that the Spanish fleet is on the retreat. Even Ireland, who has remained staunchly Catholic, would not give them safe harbour.

As everyone is breathing a sigh of relief, Leicester retreats to Buxton. He has been feeling unwell for quite some time, but even so news of his death at such a crucial time leaves everyone from the queen to the kitchen staff in shock.

My father returns to his London house looking as if he is on death's door himself. As soon as the servants are dismissed he loses his proud stance and allows himself to slump over. He takes a step toward me, but he sways from the effort.

"Father!" I rush to help him into a chair by the fire. He is shivering and I wonder if he has a fever. A hand to his forehead tells me it's not that.

"They are all slipping away." His words are spoken so softly I might have imagined them.

"Father?"

He looks at me, forcing himself to smile. "I am well. Just grieved at the loss of good men who would further the cause I have fought for my whole life."

I pull up a stool and sit in front of him, ready to jump at his every wish. My father was never a soldier, but he was never one to give in to failure and defeat like this either.

"We have won a glorious victory. Beyond all hope the Spanish have been defeated. I know Leicester's death affects us all, but..."

"He is one of many. One day I will be gone and Cecil too. Who then will stand to defend the queen? These new men do not have the heart for it." He is shaking his head.

Unbidden, Essex comes to mind. "There is the Earl of Essex. He loves the queen."

"Do you really think so? Or do you think he loves what she can give him? You have seen and spoken to him. Tell me, what do you make of his character?"

My father's gaze is razor sharp as he waits for my answer. "I believe he loves the queen. Of course, he is young and untested. Sometimes he might act rashly, but I believe he would serve her loyally. You cannot compare him with serious, experienced men."

"Should I not? Especially when we are dropping like flies."

Now I have to laugh. "There have been tragedies, but that is life."

He turns away from me. I know it is more than that. He wants to make sure that everything he has built won't just disappear once he is gone. I am not enough.

"We have won a war, but there will be another and another after that. We must be ready."

"You should rest. Now look, I am sounding just like my lady mother."

Finally, I can see the beginning of a smile on his lips. As long as I can pull him out of this dreary storm that hangs over his head, then I know all will be well.

"Frances, if something were to happen to me, you must marry."

That is the last thing I expected him to say. I tilt my head to the side.

"There won't be enough for you and Lizzy to live off of. You deserve better." He can't meet my eyes as he says this. I realise he is feeling an immense failure over this.

"I will make do," I try to reassure him. It's easy to do. I cannot imagine him gone. He will always lurk in the shadows.

7

SPRING 1589 - WINTER 1590

I am where I never thought I'd be: at court wearing a dress with a ruff so heavy I am forced to waddle. I have not gained the stamina or energy to wear the fashionable gowns the ladies wear at court. However, my lack of grace pleases the queen, for she never likes to be overshadowed.

She is watching a game of tennis, but I have excused myself to go catch a breath of fresh air outside. It's March and the air is crisp. The wind rustles the bare branches. I would be shivering from the cold if it weren't for the many layers of my gown to protect me.

I find an abandoned pavilion perfectly situated among the early spring flowers that remain defiant to the weather. Their bright hues and sweet scent are temptation enough. As I approach I hear a cough and a gasp from the hedge to the left. A flurry of grey skirts flies past me. I don't get a good look at who it is, but I am too busy gaping at the other person who has stepped out smoothing a hand over his person.

Robert Devereux, Earl of Essex.

His hair is ruffled, yet he watches me with an unashamed smirk on his face. My eyes are drawn to his hands, noting how careless he is about the way he buttons his coat.

"I didn't know I'd be coming across two fair ladies today," he says.

I am shocked at his unabashed behaviour and even more so by the suggestion in his eyes. Straightening up, I fix him with one of my most deadly glares.

He holds up his hands in surrender. "I meant that in jest. I am rather sad to have lost my companion though." Robert lets out a sigh. He's so close now I can almost feel his breath on my face. I don't know whether or not he is trying to offend me. As I try to puzzle him out, he grins. There's that spark of mischief in his eyes as he addresses me again. "I would never seek to insult you. I respect you far too much to tease you as I have."

"And yet that didn't stop you."

He inclines his head toward me as if he might place a kiss on my lips. I almost wish he would. This is wrong on so many levels. Ignoring the fact that he's a philanderer, he's also off-limits to me. The queen would never sanction our marriage. I blink in surprise that the thought would even pop into my mind, especially when it's very clear that something as honourable as marriage is the last thing on his mind.

"Don't you know you have the power to make men forget themselves?"

My breath hitches at his words. The implication is palpable. I am not used to being the object of flirtation, even though it's a common practice here at court.

"You should return to the queen before she notices you are gone."

"What about you, mistress?"

Once again he has me frowning, but at least he has stepped back. Now I can think more clearly and pretend I don't notice his handsome blue eyes or find pleasure in his musky scent. "I came out here for some fresh air. I will definitely not be returning to her side with you."

"That sounds like a challenge," he says.

"It was not meant to be." At this moment I would give anything for him to leave. I force myself to recall the scathing words I've used to describe him. He's rash and unreliable, certainly not worth my time.

"If I promise to leave, will you promise to forget you ever saw me here?"

My eyes narrow as I take a moment to compose myself. "Yes."

"Thank you." He captures my hand and brings it to his lips. "I, however, shall have a hard time forgetting you."

Not a moment later I burst out laughing, and he joins me.

"Too much?" He's smiling that debonair smile.

"A bit. You should always make your declarations believable."

He grins. "I shall keep that in mind for next time." Robert is gone before I have the chance to respond.

Conceited of him to think there will be a next time.

The queen's ladies are practicing a masque for the queen. To my great irritation it is one of Essex's designs. He always works tirelessly for her pleasure and amusement, but at the same time it is clear that he is more than happy performing this particular chore for her. What womaniser wouldn't enjoy having a troop of women at his command? I watch as his hands drift from one lady to another, adjusting a feather here, placing a hand there. He is everywhere but near me. Once, to my great embarrassment, he catches me watching him. The corners of his lips curl in satisfaction as I become flustered and look away.

In the private recesses of my mind I tell myself that I don't want this special attention he seems to be giving everyone but me. Even as I think it, I know it is a lie. Wanting him is not a crime. Who wouldn't be entranced by a handsome charismatic man? But there is a difference between acknowledging his many attractions and acting on them. I have taken note that some women will often let him get a bit too close. They will find excuses to be near him, prolong the contact longer than is necessary.

Watching this unfold before my eyes leaves me with a sour taste in my mouth. Some are married women who are definitely not free to flirt as they please. They have pledged themselves, but then again it seems that most people don't take their vows seriously. Even maidens act dangerously wanton. They would never behave like this before the queen, but they have conveniently declared this masque is to be a surprise.

One day two new figures join the fray. Their arrival makes Essex uncomfortable. It's not long before I learn that one of the men is Robert Cecil, Lord Burghley's heir. There is something odd about the way he stands, and I soon realise he has a slight hunch to his back. It doesn't help that he is already short in stature, but while no one might be fawning at his feet, no one is laughing at him either. Everyone knows he's whip smart and has won the approval of the queen. That is an impressive feat when you consider that she once sent an ambassador packing for having bad breath. The other man is Charles Blount, the son of Lord Mountjoy. The queen noticed him and was keen on promoting him to her service. He was a skilled soldier, a serious scholar, and elegant to boot. These were Essex's greatest rivals.

I watch them as they move around the room before settling themselves on a pair of chairs near the far wall.

Everyone is tense. Where once there was frivolity there is now tension. Like children who've been caught just before they were about to do something bad, we waver.

Then Essex takes charge, ordering everyone to take up their places, but not before he glares at the knowing Robert and pretty Charles.

When the queen was young and had an endless

number of suitors at her door, she used to play them one against the other.

Now that marriage is off the table, she has turned to her courtiers, who vie for the power, wealth, and influence she can offer them. Long ago there was a great rivalry between William Cecil and Robert Dudley. Now the queen is content to have their heirs inherit the old animosity. As I watch the two men eyeing each other across the room, I see she has succeeded in creating another rivalry.

Essex doesn't have the temper to hold back his anger that they are here spying on him. I can't be the only one to notice his darkening expression and the way his hands are clenched into fists more often than not. Seeing as I am little more than set dressing, I make my way over to the waiting men.

I curtsy as their ranks demand.

"Is there something I could help you with, sirs?"

Robert ignores me, but Charles Blount gives me a dazzling smile. "We were just wondering how the celebrations were coming along. The queen is curious, and though she promised Lord Robert she would not come see herself, she has sent us in her stead to be her eyes." He lingers on the word 'eyes'. My brows furrow in confusion, but then I see he is no longer looking at me but behind me. His smile is now sly.

I am vaguely aware there is someone behind me. Turning my head slightly, I see that it is Essex. His expression is dangerous as he looks from me to Charles.

"You aren't in your place," he all but hisses. I know

the anger in his voice is not for me. All he can focus on is Blount. Not too long ago, he challenged him to a duel. What could have led to matters going so far? My heart is pounding in my chest as I regard the trio of men. They are a hair's breadth away from fighting here and now.

"Apologies, I shall return to my place." I try to break the tension without looking like I'm afraid.

"We should go," I hear Charles say behind me. "We've seen enough."

By the time I am back among the ladies, the two gentlemen are on their way out and we can all breathe a sigh of relief.

When we are finished and tidying up the scenery, I feel someone watching me. Looking behind me, I meet Essex's gaze. His head tilts slightly as he motions for me to come to him. My throat closes up, but from what? Fear? Excitement? It's too much. I make to leave with the others but hang back.

I'm being a fool. If we were caught like this, there would be rumours. I force myself to walk toward the trunks filled with costumes and knickknacks for the play. Digging through them, I pretend I am looking for something.

From the corner of my eye I see him approaching. His confident saunter is enough to make my breaths shallow. Intimidated isn't the correct word for what I'm feeling, but at the moment my mind is in a haze. Just as quickly I become furious with myself. He has no right to summon me like this to his side. Nor may he reprimand me for trying to speak to his enemies. Then I go still.

What if he doesn't want to reprimand me? What if he has more amorous intentions in mind? Unconsciously, I wet my lips before I remember to be indignant at the thought.

"Lady Frances?" His eyebrow arches as he regards me.

I realise how ridiculous I look at this playacting. My expression must have gone from frightened to shocked to embarrassed. Now I settle on anger. "You wanted to speak to me, my lord?"

"What were you saying to Blount?"

I shrug. "That is none of your concern."

"Is your father allying himself with them?"

Ah, so that's what he is fearing. I clear my throat before saying, "Would it be so wrong if he was? After all, both Charles Blount and Robert Cecil are good councillors to the queen and high in her favour."

I study Essex carefully, noting how tense he has become at my words. He is a bull readying for a fight, but it will not be with me.

"I wanted to know what they were doing here." I clarify, hoping to dissipate some of that anger boiling behind his stormy eyes.

"Ah." He tilts his head. Then, as if embarrassed, runs a hand through his hair. "I apologise if I have frightened you."

"No, my lord, you have not. You have acted just as I might have expected you to act." I spin away, ready to leave, but he catches my hand and pulls me toward him. I am unprepared for the motion and all but stumble forward into his chest.

For a moment we are frozen, my face against the padding of his jacket. I can feel the soft velvet against my cheek. Until now I never realised how much taller than me he is.

The spell is broken and we pull away.

"How do you expect me to act, Lady Frances?" His words are a whisper, yet there is a heat behind them that even I recognise.

In another world, perhaps I would be the type of woman who would condescend to meeting with him late at night or in the gardens. But I am not that person. I could never let myself be.

"I expect you to act recklessly."

His smile falls away. Now I fear how he might respond to the challenge in my voice. We are alone. Perhaps he will reach out to grab me again and demand further explanations. I hate that the thought thrills me. So instead I flee back to the safety of the queen's rooms.

Like a coward I do my best to never be around him and never attract his attention again. I've been living at court long enough to know he's a great philanderer, and while he pretends to adore no one but the queen, he has his hands up many women's skirts. I will not be another of his conquests.

~

In the end, I don't have to fear. As suspected, Essex has proved to be his own undoing. My poor father is in distress. First, he had the council intervene to stop yet another duel he was a part of. Then the queen, angered that Essex would once again try to embark on a course of action she forbade, demanded he repay some debts he owed to the crown.

Predictably, he responded with equal fury. The queen had forbidden him from joining Drake's mission to destroy the rest of the Spanish fleet. So he disobeyed her commands. Once again he flees in the dead of night, stowing away on Sir Roger Williams' forces. By the time the queen gets wind of it, he was already out on the sea.

She writes to her commanders and sends him letter after letter expressly forbidding him to join the fighting. This he also ignores.

I am reading reports of the events to my father. He is now too weary to read them himself. His head aches and his stomach causes endless torment. He is having a hard time eating anything. While the whole family worries, Francis Walsingham assures his household that he will recover from this malady. Many wonder if it is poison that afflicts him. After so many years and endless assassination attempts, perhaps someone has found a crack in his defences.

I hate to see how gaunt my father has become. When he teaches me how to decipher some of his codes so I might be able to assist him, I am both thrilled and fearful. At least I have found meaningful work as I await summer, when I can leave court and return to my daughter in the country.

"How many ships were lost?" my father asks after a long period of silence.

I look down at the paper I am holding. "Only the one ship sank to the bottom of the sea, but there is disease among the crew. It's already claimed the lives of two thousand men."

"And it shall double before they return to England." My father's sigh turns into a cough. "Read on. This particular informant enjoys telling me the worst news first and then hides any good news at the bottom of the letter." He laughs as if nostalgic. "I suspect he might be a sadist."

I squint as I return to reading the letter. "Well, Raleigh and Essex fought well at Lisbon. Despite having no assistance that was promised them from the Portuguese. But I see nothing in this letter about the bounty they are bringing back."

The daylight is failing. Soon I will have to light more candles to make up for losing the natural sunlight. There are still piles of letters to go through. Under my lashes, I peek at my father. It will all depend on his stamina. I would rather see him rest, but the fear I refuse to voice is getting louder. I can't deny the knowledge anymore: he is dying. Perhaps he will defy expectations and live to see my little Elizabeth grown, but I wouldn't bet on it. My heart aches as I regard him. I would do anything to ease his pain.

"That's because there is no bounty." My father clicks his tongue, irritated with this turn of events. "We became overconfident. And that damned Essex. Why did he have to disobey the queen?"

"I think it frustrated him that she won't acknowledge him and favour him as she did Leicester."

My father begins to laugh so hard that tears threaten to spill from his eyes. "As foolish as Leicester was, Essex is twice the fool, and to make matters worse, he doesn't even know it."

"He is young." I am not sure why I am defending him.

My father, ill as he is, notes it as well. "He is a comely, accomplished young man who has won many hearts. But he doesn't have the political talent that Robert Dudley had. Nor the guile. Even Robert was never as conceited as he is."

I shrug. I can't argue. My hands fidget with the papers. I file away the ones that I read.

"You will bring Robert Cecil to me."

I look up from my organising. "Him? Whatever for?"

"There is much we have to discuss."

Something about the way he says this piques my interest. "Father, what business could you have with him?"

"He is an intelligent young man. There is a man with a bright future. It is a shame he has married Elizabeth Brooke, or I would have entreated his father to arrange a match with you."

I frown at that. Certainly it would be an advantageous match, but I couldn't see myself desiring him. It is not his slight deformity but rather the familiarity to Sidney. Here is another man too lost in his love and duty to ever take note of his wife.

"So you will bring him to me. I have much to say to him."

"Very well," I say, not wanting to argue with him any further.

"And tell me, how is the queen? You saw her this morning. Tell me of her moods and all that she said."

I do as he bids, though I am sure he has ten other informants more knowledgeable and well placed than myself. We talk late into the evening before he sends me to find Robert Cecil. My father has chosen a new heir.

A few weeks later I am back home. My mother has exchanged places with me, so I don't see her for long. She is fretting over my father but takes a moment to reassure me that my daughter is growing well.

"She's taking after your husband's side of the family, I think. Always pestering us for rhymes and stories."

"I am glad to hear that. I wouldn't mind if she turned out to be scholarly."

My mother hums, but she is itching to be on the road. My father's continued illness has caused many sleepless nights. I see the evidence in the dark circles under her eyes. She will worry herself into an early grave.

I try not to worry about my parents as I focus on Elizabeth and the pleasure of being away from the court with all its politics and intrigues.

Once my mother is gone I take my Lizzy, as she likes to be called, on picnics and for walks in the orchards, where I let her foolishly gorge on apples until she is green in the face. She is a precocious five-year-old. I don't know where the time has gone. Some days she sits by me in the morning and I show her my needlework. The brightly coloured thread and the way I move my needle in and out of the fabric to create birds, flowers, and vines on the kerchief fascinate her. When I am finish I give it to her and warn her to take care she never loses it. Later, I teach her how to stitch little dresses out of scraps for her dolls, but she has no patience and prefers using her energy to manipulate me into doing it.

Seeing how quick and eager she is for a challenge, I begin to look for a tutor to teach her languages, math, and the classics. Her nursemaid does her best with French and the basics of reading and writing, but soon she will outgrow these lessons. Thinking of my own love of myths and fables from antiquity, I hope she will find something that captures her attention in the same way.

Time passes far too quickly for my liking. Soon we are preparing for the Christmas season and I have no idea how the days slipped through my fingers.

My mother sends an urgent message that my father is not doing well and that I should return to London as soon as I can.

Fear grips me at the thought that I might not make it in time. I ride hard, only resting when I feel that I'm going to collapse, ignoring the pain in my lungs every time I inhale the frigid air.

The household staff moves around as if any sound

will disturb my father and mean the difference between life and death. Perhaps they are right to do so.

When a page boy opens the door to let me in, I take off my cloak and rush to my father's room, not bothering to change.

As expected, my mother is by his side, urging him to take another pitifully small spoonful of broth. It's strange to see the great Sir Francis Walsingham propped up by pillows looking so sickly and weak. Predictably, even as ill as he is, my father is still dictating to a clerk sitting by the window. He doesn't stop his stream of instructions even as I take a seat beside my mother, placing a hand on her shoulder. She feels frail beneath my hands. I wonder where my indomitable mother has gone.

She doesn't speak, as she doesn't want to interrupt my father, but squeezes my hand and gives me a smile.

My father doesn't take a break until mid-afternoon. Then he sinks back into his pillows and allows my mother to pamper him and ply him with food.

"You did not need to come," he says, looking at me.

I square my shoulders back, readying for a fight. Regardless of his opinion, I am determined not to be sent away. "I would not be a dutiful daughter if I didn't come."

He smiles. I catch the wince of pain on his face as he tries to rise. My hand reaches out to help him, but he bats it away. My father is still a proud man who hates showing weakness, even to his own family.

Later, after he has fallen asleep, my mother and I slip out of the room to speak to the doctors waiting outside.

"I think his colour has improved today," my mother,

leaning on my arm, says. She is daring the doctors to contradict her.

They avoid her gaze as they say that they think my father has a growth in his stomach that is preventing him from eating.

"Perhaps this summer he can go take a healing bath at..." The doctor never finishes what he was about to say.

My mother steps forward with such anger in her eyes she looks ready to strike him. I try to pull her back but to no avail.

"You are all charlatans. Get out of this house this instant."

They don't argue with her. Clearly, they are eager to be gone from here. My mother returns to my father's rooms, but I follow the doctors, hot on their heels. I call out, "Wait, masters, please."

One of them turns at the sound of my pleading.

"You must forgive my mother's outburst. It's a trying time. But please come back to care for my father. I know you are the best physicians we can find."

"We understand," Dr. Ambrose says, looking from one colleague to another. "We promise we will return in two days to check on him. In the meantime, try to keep him in good spirits. See if he will take the tonic we left with him."

"I promise I will. Is there truly no hope for him?"

Their dour expressions tell me all I need to know. My heart is pounding in my chest. I am filled with disbelief. Now I can imagine how my mom felt when she snapped at them earlier.

"Only God can know these things. Miracles have happened before. He is a strong man. Perhaps by spring he will recover."

"Perhaps. Good evening, doctors," I say before whipping around to retreat upstairs. How long does my father have? I can't imagine him gone. How long will we have to see him suffering like this?

8

SUMMER - AUTUMN 1590

Under the cover of night, we bury my father.

He has left behind debts so high that we fear his creditors will take his coffin or disturb his resting place. The spymaster has been laid to rest shrouded in secrecy. It's poetic that we bury him as he lived in life.

My father, the great Francis Walsingham defied expectations long enough to see the fruit trees blossom in April. He kept working until the last. Nothing could shake him from his path. He refused to stop or plan for his death, believing that if he ignored it he would go on living. As his last day approached, he began working at a maddening pace, ignoring the fact that his writing was barely legible.

Whatever he was trying to do didn't matter. Death still claimed him. My father didn't slip away peacefully. He fought tooth and nail for just one more moment, one more breath. It wasn't for fear of death or even the love of his family that drove him so desperately. It was his love of our nation and all the things he had left to do. When the three fates wove the thread of his life, Atropos must have cut it too soon.

It maddened him that he failed to be here to ensure the English throne was passed on to Protestant hands. I could have told him that no matter how long he lived, he would never truly be certain that England was safe.

My mother is inconsolable. She refuses to eat, and I suspect she might be preparing for a journey to the underworld herself. It is only her priest who can entreat her to drink some broth and nibble on some bread.

I am the only one coherent enough to run the estate. We must sell everything we have beyond a few necessities we keep for ourselves. The queen has said we will be allowed to remain at our London house until the end of summer, but one by one our other homes will be handed over to other men.

I write to my mother's relatives to see if I might find someone who could take her in. I don't even know what to do with myself, but as long as I can find somewhere where she can rest then I can try to focus on what my daughter and I will do if the summer plague doesn't claim us.

When someone knocks at our door, it is I who goes to answer it. I have let go of many of our servants. The money I receive as a widow is barely enough to keep us warm and fed.

The knock comes again, more insistent this time, and my shoulders tense. I expect to see yet another creditor hounding me for more money when there is nothing, so I am taken aback when I swing the door open to find Robert Devereux standing there. He is wearing a dark suit and an equally surprised expression at being face-to-face with me.

Immediately, he pulls off his cap and bows deeply to me. "It's a pleasure to see you again, Lady Frances. I am so sorry for the loss of your father."

I blink, trying to recover my senses. Confusion replaces the anger broiling under my skin. "Thank you. Do you wish to come inside? Perhaps you have some business you would like to discuss?"

During the last months of my father's life he only came once. That visit lasted several hours, and they sent everyone out of the room as they spoke together. By now I have seen Robert Cecil more than him.

"I would like to speak to you," he says, not meeting my eyes. "And your mother of course, if she is able."

I bite my lips, unsure if she is well enough for company today. "I can see. But please come inside." I step out of the way. I hope the neighbours haven't noticed the queen's favourite visiting our humble home.

I direct a waiting serving boy to show him to my father's old office and rush to fetch my mother. She has no interest in coming down to see the Earl of Essex, but she sends Marta to accompany me. I don't assure her that I wouldn't be foolish enough to speak to him alone.

When I enter my father's office, I find him pacing around the room.

"Your mother is unwell?"

"Yes. I'm afraid you will have to make do with me."

He nods. A curt gesture, and I wonder if he's disappointed. "If you have a message you would like to convey to her, you can let me know. I'd be happy to convey it to her."

"Thank you, but it is rather you I've come to speak to. Though, as you can see, I find it difficult."

I can see nothing amiss with him besides this unannounced visit, but I don't wish to insult him. Then I think I begin to understand. Perhaps my father owed him a debt and he's come to collect.

"Please don't feel you must be worried about my feelings. Trust me, after the last few weeks I am ready for anything and would be happy to help you as best as I can." I invite him to sit, but he refuses the seat so I remain on my feet as well.

"I don't believe you understand me," he says, sighing, and resumes his pacing.

"If it is about money, I am afraid my father was insolvent. He owed money to every lender in London."

He shakes his head furiously. "No, it's not about money. Well, not your father's."

He speaks the last so low that I think I am mistaken. "My lord?"

He approaches me, fixing me with that intense gaze of his. I can see why so many women are eager to fall at his feet. I blink, thinking I am mistaken in seeing him looking at me with so much desire.

"Lady Frances, I wish to make you my wife."

I am struck dumb by his words. Then I decide this

must be some cruel jest and laugh. “You cannot be serious.” Behind me I can hear Marta cough.

He takes a step forward, his face emotionless.

“I haven’t come here to make sport of you. I am intent on making you my bride.”

“And what if I won’t have you?” I throw back at him, ignoring my quickening pulse. The thought of marrying him is too much.

“I think you will.”

He is standing in front of me so close I catch the scent of his perfumed leather gloves. Remembering myself, I take a step back.

“Is this the way you seduce your conquests? Do you promise them marriage?”

“No. You are the first,” he says. His gaze flits between me and what is likely a disapproving Marta behind me. I can tell how desperately he wishes she wasn’t here. Meanwhile, my mind provides me with ample suggestions of what he might do. My eyes slide from his eyes down to his full lips. But reality strikes me hard.

“And only?” I cannot help but ask.

“And only,” he parrots back.

My eyebrows rise at this love talk. Over the last few years, I have become hard as beaten steel, hammered into shape by despair and loss. I learned the world is a cruel hard place for women without a male protector. My father could have set money aside for his wife, he could have been careful of the fortune he was spending protecting the queen, but instead he didn’t think of us should anything happen to him.

"Will you be my bride?" He has seen how hesitant I am. His eyes spark with challenge at being forced to ask for my hand in marriage again.

When I was younger I dreamed of being courted by a handsome knight, but now that he is here I feel closer to laughing than swooning from excitement.

"This comes rather suddenly after the death of my father, my lord. You must understand why I cannot give you an answer today."

When he takes my hands in his, I stiffen. His eyes are wide as he regards me with a plaintive look. "I swore to your father that I would protect you..."

With a sharp yank my hands are free. He can see he has made a misstep, but he doesn't backtrack. No one was in the room when they spoke, but I would be a fool to believe that my father asked him to marry me. Even if he had, we need the queen's permission.

"I have a young daughter to consider. I am not a maiden. You may have your pick of ladies with far better breeding and fortune than I can bring you. You cannot mean to marry me, as kind as your intentions and those of my father might have been. If you swore any promises to him, I release you from them."

At this moment he swings open his cape. The hilt of the sword he wears tied to his belt is revealed. I recognise it at once as my deceased husband's.

"I swore to two men that I would look after you. This is the neatest solution I can think of."

There's an edge of coldness in his voice now, as if I have disappointed him beyond his wildest dreams. He lays a hand on the jewelled hilt. I wish I had the skill to capture his portrait as he stands before me like this.

Now I blush and look down at my hands. "I appreciate the conundrum you are in. Understand that I would never wish for you to be saddled with me for the rest of your life."

"It would be no hardship for me."

It's hard to remember my reservations as he continues to look at me in that way. I look at Marta behind me. She is pale faced and looking toward the door as if praying someone will interrupt us.

"Marta, will you go fetch my mother please? Tell her it is of a most urgent nature."

Her eyes meet mine as if she is asking if I'm sure. I give her a brisk nod and she leaves the room.

We will have a few moments alone together. A thought that fills me both with fear and excitement all at the same time. Turning back to him, I can see his face has brightened with hope.

"Will you give me some time to think about your proposal? And the queen. Will she give her approval of the match?"

"I can manage her," he says, coming forward to take me in his arms.

They wrap around my waist and I feel their strength. His lips are suddenly on mine, and I feel all my concerns melt away in the feelings he awakens in me. A moment later he pulls away, stroking my cheek with his gloved hand. "I will take good care of you and your family. We make a good match. Can you deny it?"

I look into his eyes, and like a fool I believe him. Later I will remember the vow I made to the queen all those years ago, but for now I just want to believe that it might be possible for me to find happiness again.

We hear footsteps just outside the door and he reluctantly pulls away from me. By the time my mother enters the room with Marta we are far apart from each other. There's no evidence that just moments ago his lips were on mine.

"You wanted to see me, my lord?" My mother is glaring at him. She has clearly been appraised of the situation by Marta.

"Yes, but not before I wanted to offer you my deepest condolences for the loss of your husband. There will never be another man more loyal and hardworking than Sir Francis."

I can see the tears well up in my mother's eyes. Essex is at her side with a kerchief.

"I have cried too," he confides. There is genuine pain in his voice. I can't help but wonder if he's just an amazing actor. That is unkind of me, and I push away the thought.

He doesn't mention proposing to me until my mother's tears are spent. Then, gently, he informs her that he wishes to marry me. He renews his promise that he will take care of me.

My mother is shocked but can only manage to say, "This would be a match beyond her wildest hopes."

I can tell that it makes him happy to hear that. He

turns to look at me. His lips are twisted into a satisfied smirk.

"I have not given my consent," I am forced to remind the room.

My mother doesn't have the energy to argue, so she turns to him and says, "My lord, if you wish to marry my daughter I would never prevent you. Provided, of course, she agrees."

"Then I may court her?" He is grinning from ear to ear.

I am exasperated and I watch with shock as my mother nods.

"I shall take my leave of you all. I won't trespass on your time any longer." He adjusts his cap on his head and bows to us before showing himself out.

As much as I want to, I cannot reprimand my mother. Especially not when I find myself wishing I had said yes to his proposal.

~

Two days later, a necklace of emeralds arrives at my door. Incredulous at the extravagance of the gift, I return it. The following day, a box filled with fragments of the necklace is sent to me along with a note.

You are right. These aren't worthy of resting on your collarbone. I shall think of something better.

He cannot have truly broken up the necklace. The audaciousness of it is too much to bear.

I ask him to come see me.

The third day he arrives with a basket of fresh fruit and cakes from his kitchens. My mother is thrilled with the early summer cherries and thanks him.

We sit in the courtyard, Marta acting as chaperone, something I am certain irritates him from the looks he keeps casting her way.

"Tell me you didn't destroy that necklace."

"And if I had?" He licks his lips, his voice low and conspiratorial.

"Then I would think you are a fool and I would never consent to marrying you."

He laughs and reaches into his purse to pull out the necklace. "I am no fool, but I would have if I thought they would displease you so much. I know why you sent back the gift, but trust me when I say that I would give you far more than these simple jewels."

"Is this torment what I can expect of your courting?" I frown.

Again he laughs. "Would it excite you if I said yes?"

My heart pounds in my chest so loud I pray he cannot hear it. "I should save us both the heartache and just give you my answer now."

He hums, stroking my collarbone with a solitary finger. Then with a flourish clasps the necklace around my neck. The metal is cold against my flushed skin.

"You infuriate me," I whisper, hating how heated that sounds.

"How do you think I feel?" Then he pulls away before Marta can complain that he got too close. "Will you save us both the trouble and agree to be my wife?"

I play it out in my head—this back-and-forth game. He's right. Why not skip ahead to the end? The previous night I realised that my mother is right when she says he's the best I can hope for. I am neither a great heiress nor do I have great family connections. My daughter and I need protection and stability in our lives. He's the queen's favourite and an earl. Come what may, she will forgive him for marrying without her consent. The queen has forgiven him for much more. If she banishes me from court, then it is no punishment to me.

"Very well, I will marry you," I say so matter-of-factly I have shocked him.

He takes a moment to catch himself. "Truly?"

"Yes," I say.

And so it is done. The following day we are wed. It's decided that I will stay at his country estate until he can tell the queen. My daughter will be well looked after and I can resume her studies without any concerns over how I am to pay the bills of her tutors.

Essex has many shortcomings. If he were a smarter man he would seek a better match than me. His changeable nature and rash manner are not easy to forget. However, all of that will not matter if he can provide me with a good family and home.

My hand trails over my collarbone, the same path his finger had traced just days before. We might do well together in more ways than one. Yet I am not a child anymore wishing for undying love. He will take others to his bed. I must not care. My tears will not stop him and will make the both of us miserable. It would be better for me if I learn to expect little from him. I was married once before to a man so deeply in love that with his dying breath he called out for her. This time I am choosing to marry a man who, for all his inconstancy, desires me against his better interest. If we nurture that passion and work together, then perhaps as we grow old together true affection will bloom between us.

I stop laughing at myself. Have I not wondered this before? I will never learn.

My mother is happy that things have turned out so happily for me. Perhaps she thought I'd be doomed to living as a companion to someone for the rest of my life.

The moment we finish saying our vows, Essex pulls me into his bedroom without preamble or ceremony. He unties the laces of my gown with steady hands, muttering how beautiful I am as he plies me with kisses. I find that I have missed the company of a man and am glad that I am no longer a shy virgin.

We find happiness in each other's arms and then he rolls out of bed, pulling on his jerkin.

"You are leaving?" I stretch out, my eyelids heavy.

"I would rather stay at your side, my lady. We have unfinished business, you and I."

My skin is hot at his words, but I try not to let myself show it. I must not let him get under my skin. This is merely a business arrangement that suits us both.

"So where are you going?"

"To speak to the sun." Seeing my irritation, he is quick to add, "I must tell the queen of our marriage."

Pulling the bedsheet up to my chest, I shoot up.

"It's too late now for modesty, my lady." He shoots me a furtive smile and comes to my side of the bed. He plants a kiss on my lips.

"You can't. She will be furious. Shouldn't we keep this marriage secret? Or approach this in a—different manner?"

He regards me with a smile. "Where's my brave Frances who didn't quake when she stood before the queen? Trust me, I know how to manage her."

My smile is strained. I know that I cannot stop him even if I wished to. Besides, he is right. What can the queen do to me?

"And if she throws a tantrum and sends me from court, then I shall be free to join you and introduce you to my family."

"I would like it if you could come with me anyway. I don't know if your mother would approve of me."

He places his hands on his hips. "And why wouldn't she? You were my choice."

I want to say because he could have made a more advantageous marriage. Or that perhaps she had a marriage for him in mind already. But instead I placate him with a smile and laugh. "I'm sure you are right. I hope I can live up to her expectations."

"When you give me a son, Frances, any complaints she will have will die in her throat."

"A son?" We are speaking of children so soon? Then I begin to fear, what if I fail to give him one? His lips are back on mine, and his hands tilt my head back to deepen the kiss. After a moment he groans.

"I shall return," he says, his voice hoarse. "We shall speak at great length about how we shall go about getting you with child."

I bat him away, but he springs back with a boyish grin. "Shall I count the ways..." He recites poetry to me so loudly I am sure the whole household can hear as he retreats from my room and my reddening face.

I curse him for acting like a fool, but I would be lying if I said my heart wasn't beating just a tad faster.

Not long after he leaves, I summon a maidservant to draw a bath for me. I change into a fresh gown that would be good enough for court if it comes to it. There are several hours of anxious waiting with my mother. She is unconcerned as she reads from her Bible. Checking on Elizabeth, I see that she is fast asleep after a day of excitement. I instructed her nursemaid to let her eat as much of the plum cake and sugar confectionery as she wanted. It was a special day.

A whole day passes before my husband returns. I am watching the setting sun, trying to hide my concern, when I spot him riding home. I greet him at the doorway. His face is serious, but he manages a smile for me.

"How was the queen?" I venture to ask.

"Horribly distressed by the news."

"Ah." My heart is pounding from fear.

"She will have forgotten it by tomorrow." He is rather smug as he says this.

I touch the cuff of his sleeve. "Are you certain?"

There's a spark of fury in his eye. "I think I made my point. It's she who has to apologise to me."

For a moment I am stunned and pull away from him. "What do you mean?"

Nonchalant as always, he shrugs. The irritated look that crosses his features dissipates the longer he looks at me. I allow Essex to pull me closer to him as he pulls off the cap covering my hair, allowing the dark walnut locks to fall down my back.

"She thinks I am the sort of man who can be controlled. But I have shown her I am nothing of the sort."

My throat goes dry at his words. So he has married me only to prove a point? I am so thankful that this marriage is binding. Otherwise he might be just as keen to drop me tomorrow as he was to marry me yesterday. I try not to think about it.

His hand is buried in my hair. He tilts my head up to look at him. "Why the long face? Are you not glad to see your husband?"

The corners of my lips twitch. "I am pleased."

He tuts. "I thought we wouldn't lie to one another. But I have thought of a few ways to bring a smile to those lips of yours."

My breaths come short at the desire in his eyes. No man should be allowed to be this enchanting. But he is my husband. There is no danger here. Why not reap the rewards of our marriage? I follow him to his chamber, where he bolts the door and swears we shall not be disturbed.

A week after our wedding we receive a visitor at our London home. I am still trying to make plans for my mother to return to Kent and for my own departure back to the country.

The house is not ready to have any guests, but Essex is unconcerned, and when he sees who is at his door he can barely hold himself from smirking.

Robert Cecil steps into our great hall, his expression blank as he does a quick survey of the room.

Somehow I think he finds something wanting. I move forward to greet our guest, but Essex's hand on mine stops me. Before I can wrench myself free, Robert is standing in front of my husband. Despite his much shorter height, there is something commanding about his presence that dwarfs my husband.

"I hear congratulations are in order, Lady Frances," he says, his eyes never leaving my husband.

"Yes, thank you." I want nothing more than to look down at my feet as I used to when I was a child. I feel thoroughly reprimanded by that single statement.

He pulls out a letter from his pocket, handing it to my husband.

"What is this?" he says. His tone is needlessly impetuous.

I close my eyes to stop myself from speaking out.

The two men are shooting daggers at each other, but at last Robert says, "The queen bade me deliver you this letter myself. She demands you return to her side immediately. You have your duties as her Master of Horse to look over. If you will not, then she will give the honour and the income it brings to someone else."

My husband's sharp intake of breath takes me by surprise. He rips the queen's letter in half. I am teetering on my feet. I want nothing more than to reach down and pick up the pieces.

"You may tell her I shall return. But anything her majesty has to say to me she can say to my face."

Robert's eyes widen in surprise. But I can tell he is happy to have goaded my husband into fury so easily. "You would insult the queen by tearing up her letter like this?"

"Me?" He shakes his head. "Never. But I will not trust you to have carried anything from her to me. This has nothing to do with you. If you want to play messenger, then go back and tell the queen I will return this very evening."

I catch the twitch in Robert's hand. I can feel how desperately he wants to react, but he catches me watching him. He turns to me with a slight bow of the head.

"The queen bid me tell you that you are to stay away from court. She is angered by your marriage."

"But not enough to never see my husband again?" I cannot help commenting.

He smiles, inclining his head. "It's her wish you are to go to the country."

"That will be no hardship to me," I say without thinking. Then, catching myself, I add, "As I would do anything to make amends for any distress I have caused my queen."

"I shall take my leave," he says, and with a swirl of his cloak he is marching out of the room, his steps heavy.

Once he has left, Essex turns to me. "You cannot be upset that I will not be accompanying you to the country. The queen has summoned me. I wish she would allow you to be one of her ladies. I could ask it of her. Then we would never need to be parted."

Those are kind, empty words. Words a seducer whispers to his lady.

"I swear I shall not be upset."

"Ah, I knew you were an angel of a woman." He kisses me before pulling away. "I don't deserve you. Farewell, I shall write to you."

I watch him go, thinking that this is the only thing I can agree with him on today: he doesn't deserve me. I go to bed that night thinking I have made some grave misstep in marrying Essex. As determined as he was to marry me, I could have delayed and found a way to refuse him.

I will be glad to be going away from him. My mind will be occupied with settling my daughter into our new home and I will learn to relax. At least that is my greatest hope.

~

Wanstead House is grand and obnoxiously decorated. As a former royal manor this comes as no surprise. Still I am shocked by the expense. Essex is an earl, but I know that it's the queen that supplements his income. After getting the lay of the land I set about looking over the household ledgers. I discover they are kept so badly that I write to my husband for his permission to fire half the clerks and the steward managing his lands.

He replies that he trusts my judgment.

In this marriage, I seem to be on equal footing with my husband. At the very least, he is willing to let me take the lead in certain matters.

By the end of autumn, I discover I am with child. Distracted as I was by the work of organising the household, I have not kept track of the dates. A honeymoon child. How glorious. With Lizzy now needing me less and less, I find I have been missing having a baby around the house, so I write to tell my husband the news with a gladness that surprises me.

One evening I tell my daughter the news.

"I shall finally have someone to play with," she pipes as I am running a comb through her generous head of hair. She has inherited her father's jet-black hair.

"You might have to wait for that. Babies are small at first. They take a long time to grow."

I can see her impatient frown. The little dimple that appears reminds me of her grandfather.

"Ouch, Mother!"

I look down to see I have yanked the comb through her hair too hard on a knot. "Apologies. I was lost in thought."

"You do that a lot. Is it the baby?"

"Maybe," I say, though I truly don't know if that is the truth. My heart is heavy and full of sadness over the loss of my father. He was such a pillar of stability.

"I won't ever have a baby or marry," she says. "I'll be like the queen."

I laugh. "She had plenty of suitors vying for her hand in marriage. Regardless, her life has not been an easy one, and you are not a queen with a kingdom to rule. One day some dashing young man might catch your fancy and you will want to start a family with him. Don't worry about deciding now. You have plenty of time to think about what you want to do." I want to promise her I will look after her, but I hold back from making that statement. The future is so uncertain I don't want to give her false expectations.

"What about Aunt Margaret? I could be like her. She writes books and everyone always praises her."

A twinge of envy fills me at my daughter wanting to be like someone other than me. "If you want to, you may."

From her sigh this is clearly not the response Lizzy is expecting. I smile to myself. My little daughter is desperate for a fight or a debate. When I am done combing the knots out of her hair I set about plaiting it, and then I watch her say her prayers and go to bed.

What are my hopes for her future? I cannot be certain. I am merely glad to see her smiling and healthy. If she were to take after her aunt, that would not be a terrible thing. Perhaps next summer Lizzy could spend a few months under her tutelage as a maid-in-waiting. It might do her good.

The following day Essex surprises me by arriving in person. He holds me up, spinning me round as if we have been dancing a galliard.

"My brilliant wife," he exclaims, setting me down.

I laugh until there are tears in my eyes.

"You came all the way from London to tell me something I don't know?"

In response to my teasing he taps my nose with a gloved finger. "No, I also came to give you this."

His lips are upon mine before I know what is happening.

We have three blissful days together. I forget all about his behaviour and my worries. He has the power to make me forgetful, but I try my best to keep a part of myself tucked away. My heart will never be safe with him, no matter how much he claims to love me and sates my desires.

9

SPRING 1591 - 1592

In a new gown of crimson I await the arrival of our distinguished guest. We have decorated Wanstead with laurel wreaths, and musicians and actors occupy every bed there is available. My husband has spent a tidy fortune entertaining the French ambassador.

Upstairs, our first son, Robert, is sleeping in his cradle, but when his father arrives he will be brought down and shown off to the ambassador in a fine white linen gown. I only pray he will be in good spirits. Lizzy is with her aunt, and I am glad she is not here to witness our home being turned upside down.

I can hear my husband's loud booming voice before I see him. As the doors to our great hall are flung open, I count at least fifty guests. He entertains as richly as a prince. Even here I have heard the rumours that laugh at his pretentious behaviour. If anything could be proven, he would be the descendant of a king's bastard. Hardly a suitable candidate for the throne.

Over the next three days we will spend the equivalent of a quarter of my yearly income. Something I find hard to stomach, but he assures me that it will benefit us in the long run.

Now he leads the French ambassador to greet me.

I am not the sort of woman who enjoys being the centre of attention, but I have grown far more confident and self-assured in myself. It's not hard to smile at the tall ambassador that dwarfs even my husband.

"Allow me to introduce you to my wife, Frances, Countess of Essex." My husband holds out his hand and he draws me closer to Beauvoir la Nocle, the French ambassador, as if presenting me on a plate.

"Enchanting." Beauvoir sweeps me an elegant bow. His green eyes study my face. "I have long heard of your great beauty. I see it is an understatement."

I can feel my husband tense. I peer at the ambassador under thick lashes, lazily accepting the compliment with a nod.

He grins. "It's no wonder he cannot stay away from you."

This is a light jab, whether or not he knows it. Essex can in fact stay away from me quite easily. I find I am never at the forefront of his mind or his desires. Not long after I discovered I was pregnant, news reached me that my husband had recently become a father himself. His mistress had given him an illegitimate son. I was surprised to find that this didn't wound me as much as the fact that he must have known she was pregnant before he married me. Nor does he seem interested in his by-blow. I couldn't have tolerated the embarrassment of raising the child here at Wanstead or one of his many other houses, but Essex merely paid off the mother with a lump sum and by all accounts never spoke to her again. I doubt he even held his child once. It says a lot about the type of man he is.

I realise I have been quiet for far too long, so I force myself to smile. "It can be tiresome, sir, but I am grateful to have such a loyal husband by my side."

I look to my left and signal to the steward to begin the festivities.

We feast and dance late into the night.

My husband commends me for being a wonderful hostess. Ever since the news of his mistress reached my ear, he has been walking on eggshells around me. My opinion, never great to begin with, has definitely soured and he can feel it. Above all, he wants to be adored, and I can only pretend for so long.

"Thank you, dearest heart." I give him my most brilliant smile, aware that, sitting on his left, the ambassador is watching us.

He invites me to dance, and without hesitation I accept his hand. Essex spins me around the dance floor, leaving me breathless. His touch reignites fire beneath my veins. I know that for him this is all a bit of playacting.

Can the ambassador see how virile he is?

This whole charade is to show Beauvoir that he should support my husband in his quest for a military command. The queen has refused him but with the support of the French he might finally achieve his ends.

For once our queen is eager to go to war to support the new French king, Henry of Navarre, whose religion aligns so neatly with our own. If he manages to keep his throne, for once we might be able to mount a unified front against the ever-present Spanish threat.

I would hazard a guess that Beauvoir finds my husband amusing, but I try to keep my opinions to myself. The last thing I want is a tempestuous marriage. Despite everything, I still want a happy family life.

That night, when Essex knocks at my bedroom door, I let him in.

"Sweetheart, I have missed you," he says, burying his head in my loose hair.

"Have you been well?" I ask, stroking his newly grown beard. We are becoming strangers to each other.

"Not without you at my side. I wish you could come to court with me."

"I prefer it here." As I speak I can see the disappointment in his eyes. He expected me to love court and politics as much as him. Clearly, we have both failed each other. "Your son keeps me busy enough. But I find it hard to live without you nearby."

He grins at that. "How is that little imp? Ready to learn how to joust?"

I chuckle. "You might have to wait a bit longer for that. But he has the most lovely laugh. You should hear him."

Essex kisses my forehead. "I will, but now I would like to hear you laugh."

I swat at his hand that is moving to open the laces of

my gown already. "Really, my lord. You'd think you would let me rest after the headache you caused me with these celebrations. I don't know how we will pay for everything."

"Don't worry yourself over such a trifling amount. I will borrow money if I have to."

Knowing the state my father left us in, I cannot help but frown. He should be safeguarding his fortune for his heir. However, I cannot sully this homecoming with my misgivings. I will work on him slowly and bring him to heel where finances are concerned. So at last I soften to his advances and let him pull me to bed.

~

After three days of lavish eating and entertaining I collapse in a heap of exhaustion. For once I am grateful for the empty house and eagerly I set about preparing the household for the summer ahead. If there is sickness or plague I should ensure that our home is well stocked with medicines.

Lizzy returns to me in July with a head full of stories about her adventures at Wilton House. She speaks of nothing else but the plays her aunt has taken her to and the translations and manuscripts she has shown her.

"Did you know she's working on finishing Father's work on the translations of the psalms?"

"No, I hadn't been aware," I say. In truth I have not kept up a correspondence with Lady Mary Sidney. After Philip's death she sent me brief letters and I haven't heard much from her since. The whole family was devastated that their rising star was taken away from them so soon. I'm sure a part of them resents the money I draw from their estate. I try not to think of it or let myself feel guilty. After all, they agreed to our marriage contract; this was always a possibility.

We settle back down to our routine when a messenger arrives from court. I think it's from my husband, but I find instead that it's from Robert Cecil. With some surprise I tear into the letter only to drop it in surprise.

I cannot believe the words written there. After a moment to collect myself, I reread the letter. After he begged on his knees for hours, the queen agreed to let my husband take a force of his men to France to help the French king. I had heard about this. What I hadn't heard is that my husband has by now landed in France with a force of four thousand men.

He has not written to me in over a month. The least he could have done before going into battle was to come say goodbye. Even a short note would have sufficed.

The letter crumples in my hand as I tighten my grip on it. The satisfying sound of paper crinkling is followed by loud ripping noises as I tear it to shreds.

I can accept his infidelity, his rashness, and abrupt ways, but I cannot accept this insult. He doesn't respect me. If I disappeared tomorrow, would he even notice?

I bite the inside of my cheek as one of my lady's maids comes to check on me. The last thing I want is for her to spread gossip that she has caught me in a rage or, worse, crying.

"Can I help you with something, my lady?"

"See that this letter is burned." I point to the rubbish at my feet and return to my bedchamber, where I lock the door behind me.

For the first time in my life I find myself in such a rage I want to hit something. The urge to destroy something overwhelms me to the point I think I'm going to go insane.

I scream into my pillow so no one can hear. My fist shoots out and hits the mattress with a loud thud. I don't know how long I keep at this. The next thing I know, I am awakened by a soft knock at my door.

Standing up, I try to take account of myself. My headdress lies discarded on the floor, and the bed is a mess of sheets and pillow. I try to clean up as best as I can before opening the door.

"It's dinnertime. We didn't want to disturb you," my lady-in-waiting, Anne Grieves, says in a soft voice as if she fears me.

Taking a slow deep breath, I say, "Thank you. I am unwell. You may all go take your suppers in the great hall. I will retire for the evening. Send someone to help me undress."

"And the children? Will you see them?"

I have made it a habit to say good night to them every evening. "Of course," I say, knowing that I will have to collect myself before I subject them to the remnants of my anger.

The queen gave in to Essex after he spent two hours on his knees. Well, I shall never give in to him again, even if he spends double that amount of time prostrated before me. But that too is vanity. My husband will likely not even bother apologising or even realise he did something wrong.

~

Not long after I learn of his departure I send a letter to him in France. I don't expect a reply anytime soon. The country is at war and he keeps defying the queen's expectations.

I pack up my family and move us to Essex House in London to be closer to the gossip and news that stream in from the ports. I am with child again and find myself resenting the condition I find myself in. It takes everything in me to keep myself steady.

My entreaties for news finally reach my sister-in-law, Penelope, married to Lord Rich. She is not exiled from court as Dorothy is and can give me all the latest gossip. Finally, she visits me, taking in the swell of my belly with one surprised look.

"How are you?" she says, sitting herself on the divan across from me.

Like Essex, his sisters are beautiful with classical features that draw you in. But I find beauty repulsive at the moment. "I am as well as I could be. Is there any news of where my husband is now?"

"Does he not write to you?" she says, clearly perplexed.

"Not since he arrived in France," I say, settling on a half-truth.

"He's gone to join with the French king's army in Compiegne. Initially, he was to go to Rouen with his men, but war is changeable. You never know where you will be from one day to the next."

I fix a steady gaze on her and she suddenly seems to recall that I was in Flushing not too long ago. Mere miles away from the battlefield.

She covers her discomfort with a cough. "Of course, you'd know that. You cannot possibly be upset with him."

"No, I'm not," I say easily, for I am far more than upset with him. "I am happy to hear he is well though. He must be so happy that he has the military command he has always wanted."

"Yes, the queen really should have given it to him sooner. He had to promise he would fund the campaign himself..."

"What?" I snap at her. "He received no help at all from the queen?"

Penelope shakes her head, her mouth parted open in shock. "I thought you might have known."

"No, I was not aware." I force the words out through gritted teeth. I cannot believe this. We are in so much debt already. Only the queen's favour and her continued assistance keep the creditors at bay.

"Don't worry." Penelope kneels at my feet, taking my

hand in hers. "We loaned him the money. Did he not tell you?"

Another thing I didn't know about. I close my eyes, saying a silent prayer for patience. "No, I don't believe I know anything. Beyond his love of war."

She squeezes my hand in a reassuring fashion. I can tell she is embarrassed. "My brother is a passionate man. He has dreamed of the battlefield for so long."

"I don't know why this should surprise me." I can no longer hold back the tears and they trail down my face and hit our joined hands. To her credit, she doesn't pull away.

"Look at how insensitive I am. How could I forget that Sir Philip, God rest his soul, perished on the battlefield? No wonder you are so distraught. I will write to my brother and admonish him for his ill treatment of you."

"Thank you." I don't bother correcting her.

After that display she doesn't linger longer than is polite. Robert is brought to us, awake from a nap and babbling incoherently. He plays with a brooch in his aunt's lap as she coos over his blond curls and delicate features.

"He takes after my brother," she says.

Normally, I would be pleased, but I find it hard to stomach. My darling Robert is nothing like his wayward father.

As time drags on news finally reaches me of Essex's progress. The French king did not ride to Rouen but rather went to Dieppe. Essex, disobeying the queen's command, followed the French king. News of illness among his soldiers spreads even to us. I pray he will not catch his death out there. I am not ready to be a widow yet again.

Then in October, against his commission and the queen's inclination, he knights over twenty men. I can only imagine her fury. In this moment, she and I are very much alike. Essex is infuriating and foolish.

Even when the queen recalls her forces from France, Essex cannot bring himself to obey his sovereign. The army he brought with him is poorly led and managed. Many die not on the battlefield but from illness and famine. It disgusts me to hear of it.

At last in November he returns. Shamelessly, he greets me as if nothing is wrong. He has brought us all presents and even had a new cradle made for the baby I am carrying.

His hand is splayed across my belly as I let him hold me in his arms. "I will have to return to France. The war is not going well. The Spanish have arrived with reinforcements."

I flinch. Not once since his return has he apologised for running off without a word to me. I decide that this incorrigible man will not care even if I yell at him until I am blue in the face.

"Must you go? We will all miss you terribly."

He softens at my words. Gently, he combs his hands through my hair until I am ready to purr. "I know I'm not an easy man. I am grateful you understand me so well."

I nod, not correcting him.

It's more that life has made me cynical and calculating. It's better for my children and I if I have a good relationship with the man who holds so much control over our future. My marriage contract with Essex did not have lawyers and my father combing over every little detail. I have yoked myself to his future. It's better we continue to work side by side. Besides, I won't deny myself the one benefit of this marriage: his loving embrace. I don't even care if for him it's an empty gesture he performs for his many mistresses.

"And how is the queen?" I ask, shifting myself so my head rests on his doublet.

"I see that being away from court for so long has given my enemies time to rise against me."

"Is she angry with you?"

"I'll win her back. She's never resisted me in the past."

I bite my lip at that. There's only so much patience she can have with him. "You could try listening to her commands. She is your monarch."

"She's still a woman who's never been on the battlefield..."

"It doesn't appear the French king has done any better." I think back on all that I've heard. It sounds like his miscalculations might cost him the war and his crown. In the quiet that ensues I try to win him back. He has not come here for criticism. "But regardless, if your goal is to win back her favour, perhaps listening to her wouldn't be such a terrible thing."

"You are probably right." He sighs.

I can feel how restless he is. He feels tethered to the

queen, from whom all wealth and power flows, but he's not a man that would allow himself to be led. Trouble is brewing and I don't like it. Perhaps I will push him off this path he is treading.

~

In December, I receive word that he will be coming home.

The winter season means that the English army will have to retreat whether or not they wish to. Against all expectations, Essex has done as Queen Elizabeth ordered him. He took his men to break the siege at Rouen, and though he failed he comported himself with enough civility and humbleness that the queen is happy to receive him back at court.

He does not come to see us until January. I have gone into confinement with this latest child, and he arrives just in time for the birth of his second son, Walter.

I recover quickly from the birth and am glad to have another little babe to distract me from my husband's frustrating ventures. During this confinement I learn his mistress has also given birth and the child was taken in by his mother, Lettice Knollys.

Jealousy springs up within me, but it doesn't take hold. I have come to expect nothing less.

We christen the new child Walter, and with that he leaves us again. This time he doesn't waste his breath claiming he wishes he could be with us forever. He rushes back to court upon hearing that the post of chancellor of Oxford University has been vacated. It's a position he covets. To be honest, I have lost track of what he doesn't covet. I am only glad that there can be no hope that I am with child again. I have managed to keep him at arm's length during this stay. With two babies in our nursery and an increasingly volatile child, I have my hands full.

Not long after I see him set off down the road toward London, I see him return to me. His manner is altogether more defeated. I don't have to wait for him to tell me that the queen has denied him the post he was so sure he would get.

"Welcome home, husband," I say, laying my hands on his head as he kneels for my blessing.

"I shall receive some visitors. I hope you shall be able to accommodate them and entertain them properly," he says to me before placing a cold kiss on my lips.

The following day two men I vaguely know of appear at our house. The two brothers, Francis and Anthony Bacon, are the sons of the previous Lord Keeper of the Great Seal and related to William Cecil. What are they doing here? Surely if they should be seeking anyone's favour it would be Lord Burghley's, not my husband's.

"It's a pleasure to meet you," I say when my husband introduces them.

They regard me with serious expressions, bowing low.

"The honour is all ours," Francis says.

"Your father was a great man. We were so sorry to hear of his loss," Anthony joins in, not missing a beat.

The subject of my father is a sore one, even two years after his death, but I manage a smile. "Thank you. I wasn't aware you were acquainted." Though I wouldn't be surprised in the slightest if they were. Both these men had been living overseas attending courts all over Europe, just the sort of men that my father would love to use to gather information.

I wait, but they aren't forthcoming.

They sequester themselves in Essex's office, which has always lain unused in the past.

I suspect they are up to something, but I wait for my husband, who's never been able to keep a secret, to come to me himself.

We are watching over the children playing in their nursery. His sons are growing well and I can tell he is full of pride as he watches little Robert toddle from the chair to the nursemaid. Even Walter's lusty cries please him.

"You have given me a pair of fine strong sons," he whispers into my hair.

"A fine compliment if I ever heard one." I keep my tone light. "What of your other children? Are they well?"

He freezes at my side. Did he think I did not hear about them?

"I believe they are well. Frances, you are not upset with me? She means nothing to me. I have married you."

Perhaps he expects me to burst into tears, but I assure him with a tight-lipped smile that I don't mind.

"Sweetheart, you are your own person. I cannot command you. Know that I don't concern myself over such trifles. I know men take their pleasures elsewhere. As you pointed out, you have married me. It's our children that will be your heirs."

He is wide-eyed at my words. I straighten up and on tiptoe plant a kiss on his lips before Robert interrupts us by toddling over.

He grabs at my skirts. The gold embroidery on my rose-coloured gown catches his eye. I indulge him and let him run his little hands over the birds and flowers until he tries to pull them off the gown.

His father picks him up, admonishing him as he throws him up in the air. "You must earn your gold, son," he says with all the seriousness of a man expecting to be understood.

Hearing the seriousness in his father's voice, Robert scrunches up his face, ready to cry, but then in the nick of time, Essex tickles him, which sends him laughing.

My heart warms at the scene.

As we leave the nursery, he pulls me aside. "Darling wife, I promise you that I shall do better and learn to appreciate you beyond compare. I know that it's time for me to set aside my military pursuits. Somewhere along the way I lost myself, but now I shall prove to the queen and to you that I am a changed man. A serious one."

"Ah, is that what Anthony and Francis are doing here? Are you creating a faction at court to rival the Cecil one?"

There's a glint in his eyes as he regards me. "We

should send you out to spy for us. You are very insightful. But you aren't wrong either. Raleigh might visit as well."

I gape at him. Raleigh has been his rival for as long as I can remember.

"See, I can change." He is puffing out his chest.

I laugh. "Well, I shall not deter you from making your improvements." Trying to push down the hope that flares in my chest is an impossible task. Could it be possible that his change of heart is genuine? Will he settle down and become serious about his ambitions and career path? He could be a force to be reckoned with if he stops demanding everything like some child.

"Oh, and do you by any chance recall the name of your father's old code breaker?"

My brows furrow as I try to recall. "Thomas Phelippes? I believe that was his name."

"Thank you, sweetheart." He kisses me again.

I want to ask what he is planning but suppose it's best I don't know.

Of course, nothing is ever simple with my husband.

Raleigh pays us a visit at Essex House. I watch with hooded eyes as he and my husband play at being the greatest of friends.

I still cannot forget how he spoke to the queen against Dorothy all those years ago. Poor Dorothy, who did nothing wrong beyond being caught in the crossfire of two warring men.

I learn with some surprise that Raleigh needs our help as much as my husband needs his support. He has married Bess Throckmorton in secret, and the queen is sure to be displeased.

I can see what is going on unfolding in front of me, but with Essex's precarious position with the queen I don't know if Raleigh bet on the right horse, so to speak. However, he might not have had any other choice.

I am walking in the garden, admiring the spring flowers. Lizzy walks ahead of me picking blooms to make a beautiful bouquet for her room.

At nine years old she is already tall and comes up to my shoulders.

Raleigh approaches with a wink to me.

"I haven't had the chance to thank you for your gracious hospitality, Lady Frances," he says with a bow.

"I understood it to be implied when you spent the previous evening dancing until the early hours of the morning."

He chuckles. His eyes scan the garden left to right as though he fears we will be overheard.

"I suppose you heard about my marriage."

I give him a curt nod.

At my side he adjusts the collar of his jacket as if it's too tight. "But you will not have heard that she is with child. I fear for us both. Will your husband support us when the queen's rage falls upon us?"

"I'm sure he will."

He looks sceptical and rightfully so. I don't know if I can even fully trust Essex's change of heart.

"I will do my best to ensure he remains true."

"You are an angel, a fiery one." He inclines his head in thanks.

"Why have you married in secret?" I cannot help but ask.

"It seems like it's the only way for us."

I look up to see him smiling down at me. Ashamed, I blush. "I am a hypocrite. I didn't mean to sound as though I were judging you, sir."

"I am not insulted. Bess and I found we could not live without each other. Regardless of what the queen says, she is my wife and the love of my life."

True envy strikes at me. "I am happy for the both of you. Without fail your love will transcend any hardship."

"Have you found that to be the case?"

I never have time to answer him. My husband joins us and pulls Raleigh away. I watch the two men walk shoulder to shoulder. It would have been a lie to tell Raleigh that I believe love can survive anything. I'm grateful I didn't have to tell it.

10

1599

"Penelope, put that down!" I am shouting at my youngest, who is holding a sharp poker in her hands.

My belly prevents me from running forward, but Robert manages to wrench away the poker from his younger sister.

He hands it to me and I ruffle his hair. "Thank you, love," I say before turning to Penelope with a disapproving frown. At five years old she should know better. Of all my children she is the unruliest.

She looks at me with her bright blue eyes and looks chastened, but I know her better.

"You shall stay inside all day as punishment, while I take your siblings out for a ride in the sleigh."

She pouts and threatens to cry, but I am impassive. Penelope has played her tricks on me one too many times.

Nine years have flown by since I married Essex. Our life has been filled with moments of happiness and tragedies. I have lost three children, including my precious Walter. My chaplain reminds me constantly to be grateful for the three children I have left to me, but they can never replace the ones I have lost. I hope to one day wake and find myself barren, but here I am, nine years into my marriage, pregnant with my seventh child.

Their father is far away from me, heading to Ireland with the largest army ever to go to that faraway place. After years of working on building up his spy network, he has cobbled together a shade of what my father's used to be. He has failed to take down Cecil or prove to the queen that he is worthy of her trust.

Instead, he has resorted to hiring men of ill repute, which has caused just as much trouble for the queen as it has helped her. When he discovered that her physician, Dr. Lopez, might be plotting to poison her, he questioned him until the poor man confessed.

The details were murky, but the result was the doctor incriminated himself. The discovery of a ring from the Spanish King Philip was enough to have Elizabeth sentence her poor doctor to death.

What did that win for my husband? Official approval for his sister Dorothy's second marriage to wed Henry Percy. Nothing more. In the privacy of our apartments he rails against the queen, saying she is ungrateful. But even from what I learned about the whole affair I can see how poorly executed and thought out his actions were.

That lack of recognition made Essex stray from his path to prove to the queen what a consummate politician he could be. He returned to his first ambition on the field of battle. The capture of Cadiz will forever be his greatest accomplishment.

Unfortunately, while it might have cemented his popularity with the people, the queen has grown distrustful of him and his pretensions. Because of a vain attempt to install himself as governor of Cadiz, he failed to capture the millions of ducats waiting on Spanish ships and he led his troops farther inland to take more cities. This was a foolish attempt that predictably ended in failure. Cadiz had been taken by surprise, but now the whole country was alerted to his presence and they could mount a proper defence.

Eventually, Essex returned, but not before knighting several men, and the queen was forced to watch Essex come home to a hero's welcome. I can only imagine how that must have annoyed her. She had spent a tidy fortune on this expedition, but because of the loss of the ducats she failed to recover her costs.

The tension between them was mounting year by year. I knew the only way this could end was in an explosive fight. A secret part of me hoped that my husband would lose all his ambitions and be content living at Essex House with me.

Now, after years of being excluded from the queen's court, he has been accepted back into her good graces. I cannot help but think that this cannot go on. This assignment is his last chance to prove to her he can be a good subject. He will not listen to me. He hasn't for years, so I don't even bother trying. What money I can get a hold of,

I squirrel away in a secret drawer I keep locked away in my writing desk.

This money is my safeguard against the future, though I pray I will never have to use it.

His sister, Dorothy stays with me, and it is she who hurries Penelope back to her nursemaid while Robert goes back to his tutors.

"You need to rest," she says, urging me to take a seat by the fire.

It's March and winter's grip should have lessened by now, but it clings on desperately. I have a feeling that this child that sits so heavily in my belly will be born early.

"Should I call a doctor?" Dorothy is holding my hand, which looks so pale against her own.

I have been ill for a while now, but I doubt they can help me. "No, I need to rest. I am just so worried about what is going on over there in Ireland."

"By all accounts the queen is pleased," Dorothy says. "My husband says that the queen is content to make him Governor General of Ireland. He must be doing something right."

I nod. But how long will it be until it all goes to his head?

"Then I shall try to settle down."

"Good." She is smiling. "The last thing you and your child need is to be anxious. When will Lizzy return to us?"

"In April. She will spend Lent with us before her wedding. I have let her order whatever her heart desires. Perhaps I have spoiled her too much."

Dorothy pats my hand. "I wish my mother was as generous as you."

"Even my own was not." With a pang I think of my mother, who died not long after Walter did.

Lizzy is now a grown young woman. Her aunt took her under her wing and took her to court often. There she was introduced to the Earl of Rutland, a serious young man about her age. He was nothing like the bright charismatic knights who rode in the lists to impress the queen. Rutland is studious and composed. When he approached me in regard to proposing to my daughter, I gave them my blessing, provided the queen agreed.

So here we are. I am planning on the birth of yet another child, my eldest is getting married, and my husband is off making his dreams come true. Thus far, this year has proven to be a good one for us all.

My baby is born just as news reaches us that the queen will forgive a significant sum of my husband's debt, as he has managed to make decent headway in his campaign to subdue the Irish rebels. With the help of the Earl of Ormond, he has pressed forward through enemy territory. I name the new baby Frances and write to tell my husband that he has a new daughter.

I am still recovering in my bedchamber when Dorothy comes running into my chamber, her eyes wild and her mouth parted open in shock.

"What is it?" I try to stand but find my legs are too weak to support me.

Lady Anne is at my side, trying to hold me down on the bed. "You are too weak, my lady."

But I ignore her insistent whispering. "Dorothy, tell me what is wrong. Is it the earl? Is it Robert?"

She shakes her head. "Penelope." She falls to her knees in front of my bed with a wail. "She is...dead."

"No!" I fling myself out of bed, ignoring the terrible pain that makes my vision go black. "What has happened? Summon the doctor. Bring her to me. She cannot be dead."

Dorothy and Lady Anne force me back into bed. They are both crying. Only then do I realise that tears are also streaming down my face.

"She escaped her rooms and fled to the stables. It was an accident."

I can see Dorothy speaking to me, but I cannot hear her. My other children all died in their infancy. It is common for such tragedies to occur, but my strong little Penelope survived through that uncertain period. She was growing up strong and hearty. There is a ringing in my ears that I cannot shake off.

"I will call you a doctor. Something to calm you."

I barely register these words. What do I want with a doctor? I am in so much pain and anguish I don't know what else to do. Can't they see I don't want help? I want my daughter back.

My world goes dark.

Fire. I feel it crawling under my skin, burning away

my sanity. Trying to escape it, I twist left and right, but something is always there to hold me down. I begin to think I am in hell. What must be hot pumice is poured down my throat, and I scream for them to stop. The agony never seems to end. Endless hours, days pass me by in this torment.

Then, just as fast as it came on, I find myself restored to the world of the living. I blink. It must not even be dawn, for the two women sleeping on the pallet beds on the side of my bed are fast asleep. One of them turns in her sleep and I recognise Lizzy. What is she doing here?

Then my memories flood back to me. Poor Penelope. I feel hot tears prick the corners of my eyes. How much time has passed? Has she been buried already?

I lie back on my pillow, trying to find my strength, and push away the deep despair that is threatening to overwhelm me once more.

At dawn the household awakes around me.

My daughter is the first to notice I am lucid.

"Mother! How are you feeling?" Despite her excitement, she speaks in a soft, low voice as if to avoid startling me.

Finding it hard to speak, I shake my head.

They bring me warm broth and the liquid soothes my throat.

"What is wrong with me?" Besides my heart torn in two.

"You had a fever," Lizzy says. "The midwife thinks it might have been caused by the birth and then you succumbed because of the shock." Now she stops to hold my hand. "Do you remember?"

"Penelope is gone." I shut my eyes tight against the fresh well of pain.

"I'm sorry, Mother."

"Hush, it's..." I can't bring myself to say that it is in God's plan. "I'll be okay. How are you? And the baby?"

"Thriving. Frances takes after you." She smiles even though her eyes are wet with tears. "Don't be worried about me. Rutland has postponed the wedding. He knew I would want you to recover before we got married."

"He's a kind man. I hope you will have many years of happiness together."

She squeezes my hand again.

I feel tired and want nothing more than to sink back into the pillows and sleep for an eternity. The doctor comes and checks on me. He orders me to drink medicine and then commands me to have a diet of broth and bread for another day before eating anything heartier. Then at last they let me rest. Sleep comes easy and I welcome the black abyss.

A week later I am well enough to walk to the cemetery behind the chapel. I fall to my knees in the crypt and pray for long hours. My brave adventurous little girl. I hope she can forgive me for not protecting her.

I receive a letter from my husband, which for once is written by his own hand. He writes of his heartbreak and sorrow at the loss of Penelope. For all his faults, Essex is a loving father. He ends the letter wishing he were here to comfort me and hopes that I can find some joy that I have come out of childbirth with a new healthy daughter.

I learn from other dispatches that he is taking the army to take Castle Cahir. The lord of the land is loyal to the crown, but the rebels have taken hold of it and refuse to let it go.

Even as Essex sets a siege upon the castle they refuse to surrender. The rebels would rather die than give up their advantage. Both sides play a waiting game as they both await reinforcements.

"Do you think he will defeat them?" Dorothy is wide-eyed when I finish reading to the gathered family.

Penelope, the older of the sisters, is indignant at her doubt. "Of course he will. Our brother is the hero of Cadiz."

I have always found Penelope's affection for her brother sweet, but clearly it blinds her. She thinks ill of anyone who doubts his ability, ignoring his poor track record.

I try to shift the conversation, but we continue discussing Ireland and how he might go about defeating the rebels once and for all.

"Who knows?" Penelope says, casting a look in my direction. "Perhaps the queen will have him rule Ireland in her stead. You will go to live there, rulers of a petty kingdom."

I shake my head. "I have no such ambition or desire

for such glory. Let's see if my husband can succeed without infuriating the queen."

Ever loyal Penelope rolls her eyes. "She is just misled. Raleigh is back in favour, whispering evils in the queen's ear."

My eyebrows go up at that, but I don't comment. The short-lived peace between Raleigh and Essex ended with his imprisonment in the tower following the discovery of his marriage to Bess. Essex failed to come to his aid and so lost his friendship forever. If anything, my husband has a special talent for making enemies.

In June the English army is forced to turn back. As Essex writes to everyone, including the queen, the fault is not his but rather the lack of support and reinforcements he has received. He can't keep up his campaign deep into enemy territory without the promised assistance.

Regardless of the truth, it is uncouth of him to complain so widely and openly to everyone about the queen. I wouldn't be surprised if his letters are being reprinted on manuscripts and circulated around.

There are many in England who feel that the queen is losing her touch.

However, I suspect it is more her distrust of him that is keeping him at bay. Once again he has knighted men, and he has arrested Sir Harrington for fleeing the battlefield when the English army was outnumbered by enemies. He has also failed in his task to engage with the

Earl of Tyrone, who is still roaming free. It looks poorly that he is being so cautious holding back men in reserve. *For what?* she must be wondering.

Then his letters to me stop. If he writes, it is not to me, and none of our friends or even his sisters, who he never fails to correspond with, can tell me anything more than the fact that he is alive and well.

~

Seeing as my husband is not likely to return to England, we proceed with my daughter's wedding. My son Robert, a tall confident youth, stands in his place to lead his half-sister down the aisle.

Lizzy wears a beautiful emerald-green gown as she pledges herself to the Earl of Rutland. Around her neck I have given her the very same emeralds that Essex gave me when he proposed.

She is dizzy with happiness, and as they dance together my heart wells with pride. I wish Philip were here to see his daughter so grown up.

The couple settles down at his London home so he can be close to the queen.

In September rumours reach me that Essex has returned to England. We are staying with Penelope at one of her husband's many manors near the coast, yet despite knowing our location, he does not stop to see us nor send us a message.

Perplexed, I wait with mounting anxiety for news. I write to my daughter for news of her stepfather.

She sends a manservant who arrives in the middle of the night the following day. He has ridden hard and is exhausted.

"My lady wishes for me to inform you that Lord Robert is indeed in England. He is being held for questioning by the privy council. She says she cannot say more but that it would be best to return to Essex House and she can visit you there more easily."

I nod, pressing a coin into the man's hand.

I might be the picture of calmness, but inside I am ready to collapse from fear and uncertainty.

Penelope follows me to London. As we travel by slow stages we begin to hear news. Some I dismiss out of hand as false gossip. Certainly my husband would not be foolish enough to storm into the queen's bedchamber unannounced.

I am constantly tempted to ride ahead of the children, but my fear of what might happen to them if they are out of my line of sight is greater.

Essex House is not as quiet as I might have expected given we have closed up the house for several weeks now. Several of my husband's friends and compatriots are visiting and waiting to pay their respects.

They see my arrival as a sign that soon Essex will be allowed to return home. I try to act as if I don't have a care in the world. A day later, when I ride out to visit my daughter, I can no longer keep up the pretence. My smile slides from my face to be replaced by what can only be a strained look.

My daughter, seeing how distraught I am, takes me

immediately to her presence chamber, sending everyone out of the room so we might talk in relative privacy.

"I'm sorry for coming to you like this," I say. "I should be admiring your new home, not dragging you away..."

"Lady Mother, we will have plenty of time for that." Lizzy checks the door again before coming to sit across from me. "Now let me tell you everything I know."

I nod and lean forward in my seat so we can talk in hushed tones. I don't trust that there won't be a spy at a keyhole trying to listen to every word that passes between us.

"My stepfather signed a peace treaty with Tyrone, against the queen's wishes, and of course he fled to England to explain himself, but not before he knighted more men in Ireland."

I tsk at that, annoyed by my husband's continuous insistence that he buy loyalty and friendship with such means. Beyond upsetting the queen, he should have a care for how it cheapens the honour. If he makes every man a knight, then what will the difference be between a layman and the gentry?

"Well, he went straight to Nonsuch Palace, though there was talk that he might come riding in at the head of an army."

"God forbid." I cross myself. My daughter nods.

"Well, he did force his way into the queen's rooms. She promised she would talk to him later and, well, she did for an hour but then sent him to be questioned by the council. He was arrested and held in his rooms. They are still deliberating what to do with him."

"He's not in the tower?"

Lizzy shakes her head. "At least not yet."

I curse under my breath. My heart is beating wildly in my chest and my vision is fading to black.

"I n-need to lie down."

She helps me to her bed and I collapse on it. This cannot be happening. The queen will surely not countenance this latest betrayal.

~

This is not the time to fall ill, but that is exactly what happens. A fever claims a hold over me, and when I am not shivering with cold I am convulsing with coughing fits.

My daughter keeps me at her house, fearing that I might infect the children.

So I can do nothing but gape as she tells me by some miracle my husband has escaped the axe and is merely to be under house arrest at York House.

Throughout all of this I don't hear a single word from him. He has all but forgotten us, his family. Somehow I find the strength to get up on my feet again. Returning to Essex House I find Robert pacing his rooms, a bundle of nerves. I don't waste my time with questions or words. I wrap my arms around him as though he were a young child. He convulses into tears as I hold him tight.

"Is my father a traitor? Will he come home?"

The questions could be easily answered, but I don't have the strength to lie to him.

"I don't believe he is, and I hope so. The queen is merciful. I will try to speak to her. Don't worry, you will always have me."

His sobs subside and at last he is still. My son might look like his father, but he has inherited his sombre personality from me. I stroke his cropped hair, wondering at how quickly he went from a small baby I could hold in the crook of my arm into this young man. I pity him. He should be busy with his tutors and learning to ride. He shouldn't be concerned with his parents' affairs.

The following day I dress in a dark grey gown and plain headdress to go petition the queen for my husband's release.

I am turned away by Robert Cecil, who tells me the privy council is still deliberating over his fate. They will question witnesses on his conduct and submit a report to the queen.

He is walking away from me when I call out, "There can be no excuse for his actions upon leaving Ireland, but I don't believe he had any ill intent. We, his family, depend on him."

His expression is grave as he turns back to face me. "Then he should have had a better care of you. The queen knows you are not to blame. That much I can promise you. It is well known how little attention he pays his family. You need not fear being questioned." Then his eyes widen as he spots someone behind me.

"Lord Richard Burke, you have arrived." He inclines his head. To me he says, "I am afraid you will have to excuse me."

As I step aside with a small curtsy, I catch the newcomer examining me. What must I look like? I know my pallor is still sickly and I am certainly not even dressed as a countess. He must be thinking that this cannot be the wife of the Earl of Essex. I force myself to meet his gaze. Then I recall that Burke is the name of the Earl of St. Albans. He has come from Ireland to testify about my husband's conduct.

I march away with my head held high. Even now, after I have been brought so low, I do not want to let the world see how afraid I am.

~

My husband is allowed to send me a letter, which I read with witnesses all around me. I am sure that Cecil has already combed his words for any hidden meaning. He would not believe me if I said my husband has no talent for secret messages. We have never stayed up late into the evening coming up with a code to send messages just between the two of us. I suspect he has little respect for women, and the last few years he has rarely bothered to send me news of his whereabouts and plans. I often discover from his family that he isn't even on English soil.

His letter reads out plain enough:

Dearest wife,

I hope you and the children are well. I am sick with grief at the thought I disobeyed the queen's orders. Do not fear for my health and safety. I am being kept in honourable confinement at York House until the queen lets her pleasure be known. It is her command that we let go of a third of our household staff. Obey her in this and all other things.

Your loving husband,

Robert Devereux, Earl of Essex

I fold up the letter, my smile strained as I regard the gathered servants standing behind the queen's men. One of them takes the letter back from me. Out of extreme caution I am not allowed to keep it. I imagine it will be destroyed or used against him if he retracts any of his words or becomes forsworn.

I learn my husband has been placed under the custody of the Lord Keeper. He will not be allowed visitors and can only keep two servants with him. The queen is seeking to humble him, hoping that he will learn humility, but I think even this will not be enough.

Then I hear my husband has fallen into a deep depression; he barely eats and cannot sleep. Pity stirs in my heart for him, and I pray he will be released or that otherwise his misery will come to an end.

The queen herself sends doctors to him, and a messenger from Cecil comes to tell me I am allowed to visit him at last.

Fearing he is succumbing to his illness, I ride with all haste to York House. The mood in the city is angry. The people scowl at the queen's guards escorting me but cheer when they see me and recognise the livery of my servants.

I try not to acknowledge them. Everything I do is being watched and will be reported. They cheer for the hero they have built up in their minds. I doubt they would cheer if they knew the real man.

Outside his rooms, I speak first to the team of doctors the queen has sent. They all bow to me and try to assure me they are doing their very best.

"I am certain you are. Please thank our majesty on my behalf," I force myself to say.

They unlock the door to his chamber and I step inside the small room. Pillows prop him upright on a small bed pushed up against the wall. I am happy to note that he has fresh clothing and a fire is keeping the room sufficiently warm. Looking at him now, I cannot imagine what threat he might pose to the queen.

He blinks as if he is having a hard time seeing.

"It's me. Frances," I say, kneeling beside his bed. I take his pale hand in mine. "The queen has given me permission to come see you."

He gives a curt nod of his head. For a moment I wonder if he is unable to speak. But Robert reaches over and places a hand on my cheek.

"You came. I didn't think you would."

I close my eyes, resting my head on his palm. "Why ever not?"

"I have failed you in every respect. You have always urged me to caution, and yet I never listened."

It's hard to swallow down this apology. His words are no use to his family if he has realised too late how he could have behaved. "Then you must listen to me now."

"I will." His eyes glisten with tears. He is in so much

pain and despair my heart goes out to him. I take his hand and kiss it.

"I demand you get better. You must, not only for your sake but for that of our children and the country. I believe you will show the queen your undying loyalty and devotion in the end." I meet his gaze, watching every movement as he swears to me he will do everything in his power to meet my request.

I only wish I could believe him wholeheartedly.

11

1600-1601

My husband obeys me in one thing. Essex recovers and is told he may return to Essex House. We, his family, are asked to remove ourselves to Wanstead or one of his other properties. It is clear that though the queen is softening to her old favourite, she has not forgotten.

His trial is set for February and we wait in anxiety for the outcome. I am playing host to his whole family, and on our greatly reduced income I find it hard to keep everyone fed and warm.

One morning I awaken to find his mother, Lettice, ordering the guards to load a trunk carefully into the back of the cart.

"Take care with it," she snaps when one of them fumbles and nearly drops it.

"Good morning," I say to her, tightening my grip on my shawl. "What is going on?" I secretly hope that she has decided to return to her own home.

"I am going to try to see the queen again," she informs me, dashing my hopes away. "I have commissioned a magnificent gift for her to help soften her to my son."

The way she says this feels like a rebuke to me. I straighten up. "Are you implying I have failed him? I have written to the queen and tried to see her as often as I dare."

She grumbles under her breath. Though I can barely make out what she is saying, I catch the meaning. Anger overcomes my good sense and I lash out at her. "There is nothing I could possibly give her but the blood in my veins, which is unworthy of her majesty. Your son has spent his fortune and we are in debt beyond your wildest dreams. That is what my son will inherit from his father."

Her eyes narrow at me. "I see how eagerly you think of his death. You always thought you were better than him, but who are you? A mere gentleman's daughter whose father was not even nobly born. The truth is he is too good for you. He married you out of pity and a false sense of duty. My poor son, to think he is saddled with such a wife."

"You will not speak to my mother that way!"

I jump at the sound of my son's angry voice as he comes tramping into the courtyard. Lettice recoils at the anger in his voice.

She looks between him and me, her eyebrows raised. "I meant nothing of it, sweet Robin. I am off to see the queen to convince her to free your father. Forgive me, I misspoke."

From the way she is glaring at me, I doubt that very

much. But I don't want to continue this argument with her. The two of us watch her leave.

"Thank you for defending me," I say, placing a hand on his shoulder.

"I shouldn't have to." He scowls. "Father should be here."

"I know. I'm sorry."

"It's not your fault." He doesn't say it, but I know we are both thinking whose fault it is. The disloyal thought leaves us feeling guilty and we return inside.

The queen's council formally strips my husband of all his titles and his position at court. She also rescinds his monopoly on the trading of sweet wines, which makes up the bulk of our income.

He is allowed to receive visitors, and we move back to Essex House to be with him. Many of his supporters come to his side. We house several men and their household staff. I do not know where the money is coming from. Somehow we feed all these people and provide them with lavish entertainment.

At this point I am terrified of looking at the account books. In the evenings, my husband comes to my bed looking for comfort. Given how hot-tempered he is during the day, I try to soothe him. I whisper in his ear as we lie in the aftermath of our lovemaking to be patient, for I am certain the queen will change her mind.

He appears to listen and certainly reassures me he is

planning to be a good loyal subject to her. I stroke his hair until he falls asleep.

The next morning, I am reading in my presence chamber when I hear his raised voice out in the hall.

I set down my book and go to see what is happening.

He's with the Earl of Sussex, a bottle of wine in each of their hands as they take great gulps.

"Our misfortune all comes from that damned Cecil. He is jealous of the queen's affection for me." My husband is swaying on his feet.

Sussex is no better as he tries to clap him on the shoulder and misses. "He's a good-for-nothing charlatan. The queen would be better served if she listened to us." He thumps his chest with a fist.

"She's just as backward as them. But what do you expect of a half-blind crone?"

I cannot believe I am hearing this. "My lord husband, stop this at once."

The two men check themselves before turning to me in surprise.

"Frances! I didn't know you were up."

"My lord, it's well into the afternoon." I try to keep the anger from my tone, but I think I am failing.

"Isn't it evening yet?" my husband says, running to a window to check.

The Earl of Sussex laughs. "Who knows how many days have passed?"

"The whole of London has heard you by now. Don't you think you ought to stop drinking?"

Essex comes over to me. His arm snaking around my

waist. "You should relax. Have some." He is holding the bottle to my lips, urging me to drink.

I've had enough. Stepping away, I raise my hand and strike him hard across the face. "Stop acting like a child this instant."

He is shocked, but his eyes turn dark as he regards me with disgust. Then he spins away, storming off with his friend hot on his heels.

My hand is pulsing. I didn't hold back when I struck out at him. I wait for regret to fill me so I can go apologise, but it never comes.

We are falling apart bit by bit. We will come to hate one another before this is over. Perhaps I've hated him for a very long time.

Later that night he is sober and he does something I never expected him to do.

"I am sorry, Frances." He is holding me to him, stroking my back in tender motions.

"I should not have lost my temper like that. But you must take care. I don't want to see you end up in prison."

He nods. "I know."

I can see he is sincere, but I know how easily he can forget his promises. I don't know if I'll be able to keep defending him as a good wife should.

Our house, already full of visitors, becomes increasingly full of men who hate the Cecils and are in debt to the crown. This looks bad, but my husband never thinks about his reputation. It's almost been a year, and he thought that the queen would have welcomed him back by now. However, the Christmas season has come and gone. We are approaching February, and I don't like how serious Essex has grown. He often locks himself in his study with men like Sussex and Southampton. These are all men like my husband, shut out of court and under suspicion. They are entitled and ambitious, but they have neither the skill nor the influence to get themselves a position at court.

I wish my husband would order these men away, but he won't listen to me, even now that I am with child again. This couldn't have come at a worse time, but I promise myself I will cherish the baby regardless of the father.

Then one day I notice that more men have arrived on our doorstep. These are not men who have come for entertainment. They come fully armed and with expressions that tell me they are ready for a fight.

I cannot help but voice my concerns.

"Husband, it is time you send these men away." I say one evening.

He rolls his eyes. "I would never send someone away if they wished to pledge themselves to me."

"It would look bad to the queen. As if you are amassing an army." I catch the twitch of a smile that crosses his face. "And if you are, to what purpose? She could send you back to the tower."

He tuts. "No, she will find she is not as popular with

the people as she once was. She has started this. Not me. King James knows of my plans and supports me."

I take a step back. "Plans?"

He gives me a condescending smile. "Don't worry yourself over this. All I want you to do is to take care of yourself and the child growing in your womb."

After that conversation I learn to keep to my rooms. I keep the children with me. The last thing I want is for them to get pulled into this fresh mess their father is intent on making.

I know he is planning something terrible, but he will not speak to me about it. Outside are men with nothing to lose. My husband has promised countless things he cannot possibly deliver on. How will he improve the economy? How will excuse their debts?

On the seventh day in February, my husband receives a summons to come stand before the privy council. I watch from an open window as he refuses, claiming he is too ill to travel.

The messenger swings his horse around and rides off.

The following day, I wake to the sound of sharpening steel and horses. I jump out of bed, my heart pounding, as I think we are under attack. So I am shocked to find that it is my husband's supporters that are arming themselves, preparing for a fight.

I forbid Robert from leaving my presence chamber and make sure that the nursemaid brings Frances to my room and does not leave.

I lock the door behind me as I run through the corridors of Essex House to find my husband and discover what madness he is planning.

I arrive in the courtyard outside just in time to see four men of the queen's privy council come riding through the gatehouse. They are accompanied by four other gentlemen. I can feel how wary they are as they ride through the gathering crowds of armed men.

They unhorse, and my husband steps forward to greet them. I step up behind him, placing a hand on his padded shoulders, but he nudges it off. I catch the malicious look in his eye as he regards the men standing before him.

"What can I do for you, my lords?" He projects his voice so all can hear him.

The privy councillors wince.

Sir William Knollys, my husband's uncle, steps forward. "We have come to ask that you come to the queen to swear fealty to her. You alone."

My husband laughs. "I do not trust the intention of my enemies. It saddens me to see that you stand with them."

"I stand with the queen." Sir William Knollys corrects him calmly.

My husband falters, but then the Lord Keeper steps forward and in an outraged tone demands that all the men here clear away. "Return to your homes and cease to make trouble for the realm."

The mood in the courtyard turns ugly. Only my husband's call for peace settles them. I see that these men would have torn the Lord Keeper into pieces if given the chance.

I am truly afraid of my husband and these men. Their righteous anger drives them to madness.

I spot one of the gentlemen behind the Lord Keeper reach for his sword hilt. I meet the eyes of Lord Burke and shake my head. If he were to draw a sword now, it would be the death of him and the privy councillors.

He checks himself and lets his hand fall limply to his side.

"I invite you gentlemen to step inside my home. I promise you shall not be harmed, but neither can I allow you to return to further poison the queen against me."

"Husband, you cannot mean to do this." I rush forward, but he shrugs me away. I am ignored completely as the privy councillors and the gentlemen are escorted into the house by Essex's armed men.

"Return to your rooms, Frances," my husband says to me. "Do not trouble yourself over this." He lays a proprietary hand over my belly and nods to his mother behind me to lead me away.

Both her and Penelope are frowning at me. They are filled with anticipation and excitement over the day's events. Clearly, they are better informed than I am.

"What is going on?" I press them, but they won't answer.

I return to my rooms, locking myself in.

I try to assure Robert that all is well, but he is at the window looking out at the courtyard below. He must have seen what transpired.

"Where is Father going?"

"I believe he is riding out to meet with the queen." I shudder at the implication of my own words. "Don't worry, we are safe."

Within the hour, the men in the courtyard clear out with my husband leading them. They are likely heading straight for Whitehall, where the queen is residing. I pray they will be stopped. My husband is acting increasingly like a madman. I look at my son. I have to act to protect him. With a kiss on my daughter's head, I slip out of my room, but not before pocketing the gold I have been saving in my writing desk. Essex House is quiet. My steps echo around the corridor, adding to the eerie atmosphere. I approach the men left to guard the privy councillors without a shred of fear. They bow respectfully when they see me.

"Thank you, gentlemen, for your service to my husband. You are released from your task."

They blink in surprise. "But, my lady, the councillors are to be guarded."

"I know, and you have. My husband meant to protect them from the angry men outside, but now they are gone, are they not?"

I can see I have made them falter. It is a small victory that they don't draw their swords on me.

"He sends you a reward for all the help you have given him. I am sure he would prefer you to be with him now rather than guarding a few harmless men."

I hand them the purse of gold. I know how badly paid

they are. Only the promise of loot has kept common men such as these loyal.

I see them snap to attention at once and they bow to me again. "As you wish, my lady."

The trio stamp down the halls, arguing about how to split the gold.

I remove a ring of keys from my waist, searching until I find the right one. My hand is shaking as I turn the key in the lock. I step through the doorway and am nearly thrown to the ground by two men. But in the nick of time one of them catches me and sets me on my feet.

"Apologies, my lady, we didn't know who was coming through that door." I look up into the now familiar face of Lord Richard Burke.

I give him a curt nod and step from his grasp. The men in the room are on their feet with a mixture of confusion and fury on their faces. I can see they have been disarmed but have not been hurt in any other way.

"My lords, my husband is not in his right mind. He has taken his men and is heading for the queen. I don't know what he plans, but I have come to free you. I hope you can stop him. Either way, I fear for your safety if you remain here."

Sir William Knollys strides to me and kisses my hand. "Your bravery in defying your husband shall not be forgotten."

Shaking my head, I say, "I pray that it is. I am a coward for not speaking out sooner, but come, my lords. I have bribed the guards outside your door, but I do not know what the others might do if they catch you."

They follow me out of the room. I make certain to close and lock the door behind us. It might buy us a few minutes at least. We walk in silence and try to slow our steps so it doesn't sound as though we are running for our lives.

I lead them to the stables where they rush to their horses, which are mercifully still tacked up. The men jump onto their mounts, eager to leave this cursed place. Most set out the moment they are seated in their saddles, riding hard toward London, unsure of what awaits them. I am watching the chaos off to the side when I feel a hand on my shoulder. I am surprised to find Lord Richard Burke regarding me with pity.

"You must get yourself and the children away from here too. There will be trouble regardless of how the battle goes. Do you have a horse you can take?"

I shake my head.

"Take mine. It will carry you and your boy," he says.

"What will you do?" My mouth is gaping wide at his generosity.

"I will run fast," he says with a wink.

This isn't the time to hesitate. I rush back to my rooms, using the servants' stairs. I am shouting for my son to come with me as I am informing the nursemaid that I am leaving with Frances.

"Are you sure, my lady? Where will you go?"

"To Wanstead. I suggest you all leave too. Tell my lord's mother."

I clutch Frances to me and pray she will sleep in my arms.

Robert does not ask why we must flee like this or where the horse has come from. But he holds his sister patiently while I get myself comfortable in the saddle. I wish I had the foresight to change out of this gown, but there's no time now. I take Frances in one arm, tying her to me with a shawl to help keep her warm. Robert climbs on behind me. The horse paws the ground, and I take a moment to stroke its mane before we take off.

I ignore the cries from my mother-in-law as I ride out through the gate.

"Don't look back," I tell my son and dig my heels into the horse's side as we canter toward safety.

~

My husband's inevitable downfall starts off as a slow march and ends with the booming of cannons shot at Essex House.

His rebellion fails the moment the Londoners refuse to rally to his cause. He never makes it past Ludgate, and as the craze and confidence in his followers dies they begin deserting him.

Somehow he makes it back to Essex House, where he hopes to use the privy councillors as hostages only to find that his house is under siege. He could have tried to ride for the coast and leave England in shame, but instead he finds his way inside his office, where he burns incriminating documents before finally surrendering to Charles Howard, the Lord High Admiral.

I don't need to be an astrologer to predict the future

after I hear they have taken him into custody. I am not surprised when my husband and Southampton are committed to the tower and, shortly thereafter, tried for treason.

I am there among the crowd to witness their trial at Westminster. With incredulity, I watch my husband declare himself not guilty. Apparently, this is all a big misunderstanding. Then, madly, he continues to rail against the queen's councillors, particularly Robert Cecil, who he is sure is working with Spain. When the judges ask him for proof, he can only reply he has none.

My groan is added to the collective groan of the crowd. How can he be so foolish?

Both him and Southampton are declared traitors. Southampton leaves the court in tears, begging to be spared. But my husband stands tall and leaves without a word.

The queen signs their death warrants without hesitation. I remember how she tarried over the warrant for the Queen of Scots, though she had betrayed her and caused her harm innumerable times. The queen will never hesitate again.

I wait for Essex to summon me one last time before his death, but the summons never comes. When I ask Sir William Knollys if he is forbidden to have visitors, he informs me that he is not. In the end, Essex only asked for a priest and refused to see any of his family.

I suppose it's only fair. This time it was I who abandoned him first. I hope he knows I will always safeguard our children. Come what may, we will survive. On the day of his execution I go to my chapel and pray that he dies with dignity. Perhaps he can find peace in the afterlife.

I could spend countless hours wallowing in self-pity and filled with regret. But I cannot allow myself the luxury.

The future waits for no one.

EPILOGUE

1603

Two years have gone by, as I try to piece together a life for myself and the children. Every day I am grateful that we are alive and healthy. Robert is growing into a promising young man. Unlike his father, he is even tempered and honest – sometimes I fear to a fault. It won't be long before he is found a position at court.

A gentle summer breeze sweeps over me. I take a moment to stop and savour the sweet smell in the air.

There's something tranquil about me as I meander through the apple orchards of Sir Walter Raleigh's estate. His wife has invited me to stay for the summer months and I am happy to be in the company of such a lively woman. We spend our days walking through gardens, or riding in the deer park. In the evenings, we sew by the fire as we entertain ourselves with lively debates and giggle like young girls over gossip from the court.

I am no longer as young as I used to be, but neither have I withered away. With age has come wisdom and acceptance. I discover I can forgive the men I married for not loving me as completely as I would have wished. Considering the outcome, it was for the best. Love cannot be forced, it must be given willingly.

There is perhaps another secret reason why I am so at peace.

When I open my eyes again, I see him standing at the other end of the lane, regarding me with a lopsided smile.

"Lady Frances, good day," he calls out.

I raise my hand in greeting and study him as he approaches me.

"Good day, Lord Richard. What brings you here this day?"

"A Faerie Queene," he says, presenting me with a bouquet of wildflowers he had concealed behind his back.

I tut at him. "Should the queen hear you say that..." Then I shake my head. "What will become of you?" I step closer to him. My gloved hand on his.

He casts a glance around us.

"We are alone," I reassure him.

He hums and tilts my chin up to meet his searching glance. "This is most improper, my lady."

A sly smile spreads across my face as I'm drawn closer by his entrancing eyes. "I am grateful that such a great knight is here to protect my virtue." The flowers he holds fall to the ground as I close the distance and press my lips against his own.

His arms wrap around me as he attempts to bite back a moan. The kisses alternate between sweet caresses and pressing desire. At last Richard pulls away, though he doesn't release me from his hold.

"We cannot keep going on like this my darling, Frances," he whispers. "Have you thought about my proposal?"

My mouth is dry and for a moment I think of lying to him. But there is no lying to someone like Richard Burke, Earl of St. Albans and Clanricarde. "Every moment. You cannot imagine the temptation. But how can I? You deserve a far better marriage..."

He silences me with another kiss, nipping my bottom lip in disapproval. "Don't you dare say such things. I've wanted you since the moment you rescued me from that traitor's clutches."

"I never realised it until now but you were a damsel in distress."

"Indeed, I was even kept under lock and key." He bats his eyes at me and we cannot help but laugh. Then his expression grows serious. "You are the only one I want by my side. These secret meetings and stolen kisses — they aren't a game to me. If you will have me the queen will give her blessing for this union."

"How do you know that?"

"I have already asked her."

"Tell me you haven't!" Richard cannot know what this means to me. If I agree this would be my first marriage conducted in the open.

"But I have. So you have no choice but to accept that you will be saddled with me until we both grow old and decrepit."

In shock, I swat his arm attempting to hide the joy blossoming in my chest. "Such sweet words and promises of the future. How can I say anything but yes?"

"How indeed..." He agrees, then stops to mid-sentence. "Though I wouldn't mind trying to convince you some more." Richard leans forward as if to kiss me again.

"You are incorrigible."

Our eyes lock as he holds me to him tighter than ever. "No. Insatiable."

AFTERWORD

Two years after the death of her second husband, Frances would marry Richard Burke, the Earl of St. Albans. They would live primarily in Ireland. By all accounts, they had a happy marriage and three children.

She would die in 1633 at the age of sixty-six.

Her son Robert would be educated at Oxford, and under the reign of King James he would be reinstated as the Earl of Essex and would be a companion to the Prince of Wales.

Her daughters with Essex, Frances and Dorothy (born after his death) both grew to maturity. They were patrons of the arts and wrote poetry.

Elizabeth Sidney or Lizzy as I have referred to her in this story, would die young and without issue.

Printed in Great Britain
by Amazon

77329647R00135